"I'd *to work," Daniel announced.*

Brittney flicked him a sideways glance, full of flirtatious humor. "All work and no play, Daniel?" she murmured.

His expression changed subtly, showing both interest and wariness at the caressing purr in her voice. "So what did you have in mind?" he asked, taking up the challenge at once.

"Midnight swims in the lake, riding with the top down in a flashy red convertible, picnicking in a secluded meadow." She batted her lashes at him.

He threw back his head and laughed.

Brittney gave him a disgusted look. "You could at least be a little smitten when a woman flirts outrageously with you."

He turned her face to his. "What's this all about, Brittney? Are you trying out your feminine wiles on me?"

Now was not the time to back down. "Perhaps."

"Because if you are . . ." A slow sexy smile spread over his mouth. "I might be susceptible."

Dear Reader,

Welcome to Silhouette Romance—experience the magic of the wonderful world where two people fall in love. Meet heroines who will make you cheer for their happiness, and heroes (be they the boys next door or handsome, mysterious strangers) who will win your heart. Silhouette Romances reflect the magic of love—sweeping you away with books that will make you laugh and cry, heartwarming, poignant stories that will move you time and time again.

In the next few months, we're publishing romances by many of your all-time favorite authors such as Diana Palmer, Brittany Young, Annette Broadrick and many others. Your response to these and other authors in Silhouette Romance has served as a touchstone for us, and we're pleased to bring you more books with Silhouette's distinctive medley of charm, wit and—above all—*romance*.

During 1991, we have many special events planned. Don't miss our WRITTEN IN THE STARS series. Each month in 1991, we're proud to present readers with a book that focuses on the hero—and his astrological sign.

I hope you'll enjoy this book and all of the stories to come. Come home to romance—Silhouette Romance—for always!

Sincerely,

Tara Gavin
Senior Editor

LAURIE PAIGE

Man from the North Country

Published by Silhouette Books New York

America's Publisher of Contemporary Romance

To Tara,
who understands what I mean
and sees that I say it.

SILHOUETTE BOOKS
300 E. 42nd St., New York, N.Y. 10017

MAN FROM THE NORTH COUNTRY

Copyright © 1991 by Olivia M. Hall

MORE ABOUT THE AQUARIUS MAN.
Copyright © 1991 by Harlequin Enterprises B.V.

The publisher acknowledges Lydia Lee's contribution to
the afterword contained in this book.

ISBN: 0-373-08772-1

First Silhouette Books printing February 1991

Books by Laurie Paige

Silhouette Romance

South of the Sun #296
A Tangle of Rainbows #333
A Season for Butterflies #364
Nothing Lost #382
The Sea at Dawn #398
*A Season for Homecoming #727
*Home Fires Burning Bright #733
Man from the North Country #772

*Homeward Bound Duo

Silhouette Desire

Gypsy Enchantment #123
Journey to Desire #195
Misty Splendor #304
Golden Promise #404

Silhouette Special Edition

Lover's Choice #170

LAURIE PAIGE

has recently moved to California, where she is busy writing and falling off mountains—translation: trying to snow ski. During the summer she and her husband went camping, and she did a lot of falling then, too. Friends had brought along a sailboard, and she had to try it. As soon as she recovers from all this fun, she plans to use these experiences for some spunky heroine (who will be able to do each of them flawlessly on the second try!).

A Note From The Author:

Dear Reader,

As soon as Tara and I discussed the Aquarian man—rugged individualist, cool intelligence, iron nerves—he instantly came to life in my imagination. I even knew his name: Daniel.

The more I learned about him, the more I found to love. Daniel was a man to lean on, steady as a rock, dependable. He accepted responsibility and made wise decisions. Wonderful. What's not to love?

Ah, but what about that fixed air sign? Could it be that Daniel was also stubborn, perhaps a little set in his ways and determined not to yield an iota of his independence to a woman? And remember, a fixed sign indicates a fixed personality, a man who can't—or won't—be changed.

Fortunately for Daniel, I also knew a heroine who absolutely believes that everyone can change and grow as a person, as a lover, as a husband. It was just a matter of opening his eyes to a few truths. Besides, Sagittarians can be pretty stubborn, too. Coming from the fire sign, Brittney is determined to add fuel to the sparks that ignite whenever she and Daniel come close.

Sparks? For Daniel, it's more like spontaneous combustion.

All I had to do was get these two characters together. They wrote their own story.

Laurie Paige

Chapter One

Brittney Chapel swayed against the passenger door as the red sports car swung wide around the curve. Fortunately, the traffic was light for a Friday afternoon in June. "You'd better slow down," she advised. "If you get another ticket, you'll lose your license."

Her friend, Carol Montclair, lifted a manicured hand from the wheel with an airy gesture. "Never fear. Unca Daniel is here."

Daniel. Just the sound of his name did strange things to Brittney. Undefined anger, shimmery hot, coiled through her. He was the only person who could make her furious with just a glance from his frosty blue eyes.

"Here?" she managed to ask in a disinterested tone, in spite of the jolt to her composure.

She hadn't expected Daniel to be at the house on Lake Minnetonka. Although he owned it, he rarely went there. He preferred the logging operations in the northern part of the

Muggs, whose real name was Muggorski, was a kind, long-suffering man who answered to the nickname with grave dignity. His wife, Mrs. Muggs, was the housekeeper and cook.

"I'll see to it. Mr. Daniel is holding a meeting," he added.

The warning was lost on Carol, who started blithely up the stairs, Brittney close behind her.

Muggs, with one worried glance over his shoulder, exited.

The door to Daniel's study opened, and it was Daniel himself who stepped into the hall and silently closed the door behind him.

"Hold on, you two," he ordered, his voice carrying above the sounds of their ascent the way the lower notes of a cello carried over those of violins.

Brittney did a slow burn. He spoke no word of greeting. Not one smile softened his mouth. No simple phrases welcomed her to his home. In fact, he probably wished she would get lost and never come back. Well, too bad.

She and Carol stopped. They both faced him like schoolgirls called on the carpet by the principal. Even from the bottom of the stairs, looking up at them, Daniel was a formidable presence.

"Where the hell have you two been for the past three days?" he demanded, his eyes cold as he looked them over. "Beatrice has been out of her mind with worry."

Carol flushed guiltily. "Well, we decided to stop for a couple of days with a friend from school."

"This person doesn't have a telephone?"

He spoke softly—deceptively so, Brittney thought—as Carol apologized for their thoughtlessness and hurriedly explained where they had been. Daniel, the Inquisitor. He was the one person who could topple Carol's innate self-possession with only a word.

"We'll catch her later, then." Carol bounded up the stairs, pulling Brittney with her.

Brittney was aware of his eyes boring into her as she followed Carol. At the top of the stairs, she went into the room next to Carol's that had become "hers" when she visited, and waited for her luggage to arrive. Leaning against the cool pane of the window, she stared at the wedge of lake visible from there. She realized she was trembling slightly.

Don't overreact, she cautioned herself, her thoughts going immediately to Daniel Montclair and the brief scene in the hall.

An Aquarian. "Last of the rugged individuals," Carol had once called him. Cool intelligence. Iron nerves. Innovative. A man to lean on. Steady as Gibraltar. And without a doubt, the most infuriating person she'd ever run across!

Brittney closed her eyes, picturing him. He would have been perfectly at home in the first Queen Elizabeth's time. He belonged to the era of Raleigh and Drake and adventures of discovery upon the seven seas. He would have commanded a tall ship and navigated by the stars, and answered to no man... or woman.

She scoffed at her musings, opening her eyes and focusing once more upon the rippling water of the lake and the trees on the spacious lawn.

Suddenly, in her mind's eye, she saw him as he was: almost a head taller than her own medium height, with dark hair, blue eyes and the build of a distance runner. He was thirty-one—ten years older than she was.

Once she had imagined herself in love with him.

He possessed an intensity that Brittney found intriguing. According to the star charts Carol liked to read, he had an inner core of white-hot passion that, if one could ever penetrate the icy reserve shielding it, would erupt into a fiery devotion that would be concentrated exclusively on the person who had unleashed it.

What a foolish notion.

Still, Brittney sometimes wondered what it would be like to be the recipient of that devotion. Her imagination soared. Daniel: gentle... fierce... ardent... demanding...

Dear God, to be loved like that!

The thought brought tears to her eyes. She blinked them away. Daniel was right. She *was* all grown-up. Time to put the dreams away and be the woman she wanted him to see. After all, she'd soon be starting to work.

Her degree in fine arts had earned her the position of assistant to the curator at a small museum in St. Paul. Carol's mother had arranged the interview. However, Brittney'd had to go through the same process as three other people to land the job, so she felt she'd gotten it on her own merit.

The truth was, she'd wanted to live near Carol and her family rather than her own mother and half brother in Louisiana. Near Daniel? her conscience questioned.

Okay, so she'd been attracted when they'd met three years ago. Her emotions had rioted whenever she saw him, which hadn't been all that often since the first trip. During that two-week period, he'd stayed for dinner almost every night, had attended parties with them, had even taken the three women to the theater, although Carol said he had little patience for plays and other forms of escapism.

It had been wonderful... while it lasted.

He had abruptly disappeared, heading for the north country and the land he loved. A logging emergency, he had explained.

"Are you over your mad spell?" Carol asked, opening the adjoining door and poking her head in.

"I wasn't mad," Brittney asserted.

Carol looked as if she would argue the point, then changed her mind. "Do you want to unpack or go for a swim to cool off?"

"Unpack."

Carol wrinkled her nose. "I knew that's what you'd choose. You always have to do the chores first, then play later."

"It's better than your way. You never get to the chores," Brittney retorted.

"Just for that, I'll bet you a dime to a doughnut I'll beat you getting finished, and I have two more suitcases than you."

"You're on."

Muggs brought Brittney's cases first. She waited until Carol had hers, then they began a flurry of activity. Just before Brittney placed the last pair of evening shoes in the closet, Carol yelled, "Done!"

"I don't believe it," Brittney said. She went to the door between the rooms. "You must have cheated. Did you hang up your stuff or throw it on the floor?"

"Look and see," Carol invited.

Her closets were neat, but they didn't contain many clothes. "What did you do with your things?"

"Most of them were dirty. I put them in the hamper." Carol's smile was blatant with triumph. "You owe me a doughnut. I'll collect in the morning. We'll go to the village for breakfast."

"You just want to look over the men at the resort so you can decide who's going to be your summer romance," Brittney accused, knowing her friend well.

"Who's going to be yours?" Carol challenged, taking her bathing suit from a drawer. She pulled her T-shirt over her head and tossed it at the bed. It landed on the carpet.

Brittney's smile faded as she retreated to her room to change clothes. Who *was* going to be hers?

Not a summer romance—she hadn't Carol's lightheartedness concerning romance. What she wanted was a passionate, death-defying love. She wanted to be first in someone's life and heart. She wanted to love and be loved with the blazing intensity of a meteor. She'd rather be consumed in the blaze than spend her life in some lukewarm relationship.

A great longing grabbed her heart. She had always been filled with so much love. Her heart brimmed with it. She had always had more to give than any one person could take. Where was the man who would love her like that?

She sighed, then smiled, remembering her own youthful excesses.

Her mother had explained to her when she was still a child that people did not enjoy being smothered with kisses and hugged so tightly one's clothing was wrinkled. Brittney had learned to curb her affectionate displays to light kisses on her mother's carefully made-up cheek.

Carol sometimes reminded Brittney of her younger, less disciplined self. Perhaps that was why they had taken to each other and remained steadfast friends for four years.

"Ready?" Carol strolled in.

Brittney nodded.

Speculating on the promises of the summer, they headed for the cooling waters of the lake. Carol plunged in straightaway in her usual headstrong manner. Brittney gazed into the water, picked her spot, then dived in cleanly. She swam out to the raft where Carol lay, then turned and swam back to the end of the pier. On her third trip, she pulled herself onto the float and stretched out beside Carol to let the sun dry her.

"How can you have so much energy?" Carol mumbled, half asleep.

"I didn't help you with the driving today." The spongy mat covering the raft felt good on her back; the sun felt good on her chest. Tension oozed out of her. She grew drowsy.

"You were preoccupied." Carol grinned without opening her eyes. "As usual, when you come here."

There was a teasing, I-know-a-secret tone behind the words. Brittney tensed. "Oh?" she said nonchalantly.

"You were thinking about Daniel." Carol rolled over onto her stomach and propped herself up on her elbows. "Weren't you?"

"Why would I be thinking about him?"

Carol shrugged. "Beats me. He's such a drag, always working. But he's sweet . . . when he isn't mad as everything at me." Her grin broadened.

Brittney knit her brows in worry. Had her early feelings been so obvious? She'd tried not to act the part of the stricken schoolgirl. Had she failed?

What did it matter now? Daniel had made it perfectly clear he wasn't interested in her. He hardly acknowledged her as a person; as a woman, he totally ignored her.

That fact, more than any other, was what made her so furious! She paused, stunned by this insight. The man-woman thing, she scoffed. It could drive a person crazy.

"He can be nice" was all she said. She ignored the shimmer of anger in her blood just as Daniel ignored that which was female in her. It seemed that no one wanted the totality that was Brittney Chapel.

Her thoughts drifted to Daniel's life. Maybe he felt the same. Carol and her mother, Beatrice, took Daniel for granted.

He'd been only twenty-five when his brother—fifteen years his senior—had died, leaving the younger man in charge of their various companies, as well as executor of his estate and the responsibility of his widow and sixteen-year-old daughter.

No one seemed to appreciate Daniel's having had to give up his archaeological studies and take on the other chores. Brittney wondered if he ever resented the burden that had been dumped on him six years ago.

"Carol, telephone." A deep voice interrupted her reverie.

How, Brittney wondered, did people always seem to know when Carol was back in town? It was the strangest phenomenon.

"Coming." Carol sat up and plunged over the side. She started toward the shore, passing Daniel en route.

Brittney moved over when he pulled himself onto the raft, spraying cold water over her sun-warmed legs and abdomen. A shiver swept down her body.

She glanced at his hands and away. He had the most expressive gestures. He also had calluses on his palms from the logging work he loved and sometimes indulged in.

Carol's mother didn't like his doing manual labor. She thought it was beneath the family's dignity. Daniel just nodded good-naturedly and told her not to worry. Brittney thought the older woman was afraid Daniel might get killed in a logging accident the way her husband had. Then who would take care of her?

"Did I get you wet?" he asked, dropping down beside her. "Sorry." He flicked the water off her thigh, his impersonal touch creating a burning sensation that spread through her.

"That's okay."

She looked away from the dark mat of hair on his chest, only to encounter his legs, strong and still dripping with water.

She was so aware of him. That was one thing that hadn't changed. Even when she was furious with him, she was lured by his grave good looks, his quiet strength. Idly she wondered what would happen if he ever touched her. As if he ever would.

"I wanted to apologize for what I said earlier."

She looked at him in surprise.

He returned her stare. "You were right. I had no right to demand that you report your movements to me."

Brittney recovered her poise. "Carol and I have lived on our own for four years. We didn't realize anyone would worry."

Her voice was prim. She was still angry over his lack of greeting. He could have shown a smidgen of pleasure at seeing them arrive safely, instead of jumping on them the moment they appeared.

"Naturally we worried," he said, his expression hardening once more. "You could have been in an accident—"

"You know, Daniel, if you'd expressed those fears instead of treating us to your temper, we'd have felt worse and learned a lesson at the same time."

She felt a touch of smug satisfaction at the dumbfounded look that crossed his face. Daniel Montclair wasn't used to being corrected. Perhaps she should point out it was good for his soul to be put in the wrong on occasion? Better not press her luck.

During the two weeks since graduation, Carol had been with Brittney at her house in Shreveport while Brittney sorted through her belongings and packed for their trip. Then they had decided to stop a few days with a friend who had gotten married and dropped out of school the previous year. The friend had recently lost a baby, and they had wanted to cheer her up. Should she explain?

"Did Carol drive like a maniac on the road?" he asked, changing the subject. "She tends to have a heavy foot."

Brittney had to smile. "She drove as usual—flat-out."

They laughed.

Hearing his laughter, she was reminded of the time two summers ago when he had taken her sailing on the Hobie Cat. The wind had been strong, causing one pontoon to rise out of the water.

"Hold on!" he had yelled.

Too late. Brittney had fallen in.

Laughing, he had loosened the sail, letting it flap in the wind while she tried to clamber on board again. Finally he had aided her by grabbing the waistband of her slacks and hauling her onto the canvas stretched between the pontoons. His hands had been strong and warm as he steadied her and helped her sit upright.

She remembered how his eyes had darkened when he had taken in the sight of her, clothes plastered to her wet skin, her nipples almost visible and clearly erect in the cooling breeze.

He had caressed her waist, his hands kneading the soft, boneless flesh there. He'd said her name. *Brittney.* A warm, delicious, spoken caress. She had wanted to feel her name on his lips, to taste the sweet desire of his mouth on hers.

Just for one second, she had witnessed that white-hot passion, that fierce intensity that dwelt at the core of his being.

She had wanted to experience it again.

Remembering, she felt her breasts contract. She casually raised one knee and crossed her arms over it, hiding her reaction to past memory and present awareness. After that one moment in time, he had shut her out.

"So, how does it feel to be all grown-up and working for your living?" he asked, his expression unreadable once more. She wanted to ask if he really cared.

He had left the house the day after the sailing incident to attend to a logging accident. Since then, she'd rarely seen him. When their paths had crossed, he had played his role as host to perfection—always polite, always remote. Except for odd little exchanges like today's.

"Well, it's nice to be out of school, but I won't be working for a month yet. That'll give me time to find a place to live."

One dark brow rose in question. "What's wrong with here?"

"Carol is my best friend. I'd like to keep it that way," she replied with droll humor.

He laughed again, a chuckle of understanding that caused an ache to start inside her.

"Carol can be difficult," he admitted.

"So can I," Brittney confessed. "I suppose we all have our quirks."

"Even you?"

She thought he sounded sarcastic but she wasn't sure. He shifted his weight, moving one knee up and resting his arm over it the way she was doing. They were suddenly closer. His warmth filled the space between them.

"You've always been the perfect guest," he continued in the same tone of voice.

She was startled by the adjective. Perfect? Hardly. On some elementary level, she was sure he disliked or at least disapproved of her. But maybe she was mistaken.

"Ha," she said.

"Quiet, agreeable," he continued ruthlessly. "Ready to join whatever activity was announced, ready to suggest a plan if boredom seemed about to set in. I sometimes wondered what you were thinking. Or if you ever got bored."

His glance became speculative, as if he could see inside her head and knew her self-control was a farce. She could tell nothing from his face. Was he mocking her or complimenting her?

"It's easy to enjoy yourself here." Her gesture took in the house and beautiful lawns, the pier and lake.

A bed of roses was in bloom, she noticed, in shades of pink from the palest to the deepest. The air was filled with their perfume, not subtly but flagrantly, as if they could produce the scent forever instead of for only a season.

"This place is so beautiful it hurts." She pressed her hands over her heart, then clasped them together in her lap, embarrassed by her outburst. Daniel had a natural reserve like her mother; he wouldn't appreciate her emotional outbursts, either.

They sat in uneasy silence for a few minutes. Brittney felt him shift again. When she glanced at him, his eyes were roaming over her. Her nipples constricted painfully. He edged forward and let his legs dangle in the water. She moved over and did the same.

"So, now what?" he asked. "You have your B.A. Is the M.R.S. your next degree?"

For one wild moment, she was tempted to say, *Only if you're offering it,* just to see what his reaction would be.

He'd probably run for the north and the safety of the company's vast forests, just as she suspected he'd done the other time sparks of desire had flashed between them.

"Hey, anyone home?" He pretended to knock on her forehead. "Did you go to sleep in there?"

"Sorry. I was thinking."

"About the M.R.S. degree?"

His cynical teasing riled her, but she kept her tone light. "About work. I'll be a career woman, remember?"

"There's no special someone, no poor guy languishing back in New York, wishing you'd write or call?"

She shook her head.

"In Louisiana?"

She hesitated just a fraction before denying it.

"But there's someone who'd like to be," he concluded.

Brittney was startled that he read her so well. There had been an old childhood chum who had made it plain he wished she felt more than affection for him. He'd been angry that she was taking a job so far away. He had wanted to know why she wouldn't give him a chance.

She glanced at Daniel from the corner of her eye. Stan had accused her of being in love with someone else. He'd been jealous of the unknown man and frustrated by her decision. However, he'd been wrong. She wasn't in love with anyone, and wasn't likely to be in the near future.

She had told Stan that; but she'd also had to tell him she would never fall in love with him. She'd hated to hurt him, but, as she'd discovered long ago, love can't be forced. It had to come of its own free will. But she understood Stan's hurt.

Would her old friend sympathize if he knew how desperately she had once wished Daniel Montclair would make love to her?

"Daniel!" Carol shouted. "Your office wants you to call. Brittney, come on in. Mrs. Muggs made gingersnaps."

Daniel muttered something under his breath, then sighed in resignation. "Gingersnaps a favorite of yours?" he asked as they stood and prepared to swim back to shore.

"Uh-hmm." She looked up at him. "Are you supposed to be on vacation?"

He snorted. "That would be the day."

She sensed an underlying dissatisfaction. She'd assumed he liked being in charge of the timbering, papermaking and printing operations of Montclair Enterprises. Of course, he'd had to give up his own plans when he'd taken over; but he seemed such a natural leader.

Well, we all give up something as we grow older and face the world, she thought philosophically. She'd given up on the fantasy of his falling madly in love with her.

But, just once, an insistent voice inside her whispered, it would be nice to make him acknowledge her as a woman, rather than as a not-very-wise adjunct to his niece. Just once, she'd like to have him on his knees, imploring her for one kiss.

Daniel Montclair on his knees? Bro-ther!

"Something funny?" he snapped, apparently angry again.

"Yes. I'll tell you sometime." She gave him an impish grin and dived into the cooling waters. He dived in after her.

Daniel swam on his side, observing her strokes and easily keeping up with her, using a power kick. If she turned toward him, if their legs meshed, if they kissed...the lake would probably vaporize, he concluded ruefully.

The rigid weight of desire settled in his lower limbs. Damn. He was a man. He should be able to control his wayward impulses. The man-woman thing was more powerful than he'd realized. It had increased his anger with her thoughtless delay in arriving, he admitted. He had been impatient to see Brittney all grown-up and out of school.

But it didn't make a damn bit of difference to their situation. What was he planning on doing? Inviting her to have a grand affair and to hell with the consequences? A man couldn't seduce his niece's best friend and live with his conscience—not to mention the flak he'd take from Beatrice and Carol.

He watched the smooth movements of Brittney's arms through the water. He'd like to stroke that satiny skin until she sighed and trembled in his arms, until she was as wild for him as he was for her. Once, he'd seen desire leap into her eyes.... But she'd been too young, too innocent then.

She isn't now, his body stated, loud and clear.

She still *looked* innocent. Her gaze was the most candid he'd ever seen. And those incredible lashes. They were long and thick and curved upward in the most tantalizing way. Right now, they were clumped together with moisture. He wanted to kiss and lick it away. And then? He didn't dare think on it.

And all those questions about the M.R.S. degree. Cute, Daniel. Real cute. Next thing he knew, she'd think he had proposed. That would be the day!

He'd seen what marriage had done to his older brother. Adam's life had been circumscribed by Beatrice's fears and demands. The woman couldn't make a decision without consulting everyone she knew.

A surge of restlessness overcame him. He rolled over in the water and threw his shoulders into a hard crawl, leaving Brittney, his lovely tormentor, behind. Scowling, he waited for her at the dock. Fortunately the water was still over his waist. Its chill was cooling his blood somewhat.

He was suddenly angry—at himself for wanting her; at her for being the cause of it. Life could be hell.

Brittney swam leisurely to the shore, refusing to become irritated when he left her in his wake. When she came alongside, he lifted her onto the pier, then hauled himself up.

"Thanks," she said coolly.

With a curt nod, he jogged off, dripping water, to take care of business. She could almost see the ten-foot-high fence he had erected around himself. Dared she cut her way through?

She'd once asked Carol if Daniel had ever been seriously involved with anyone. If there'd ever been someone special, he hadn't brought the woman home or announced an engagement or made plans for the future.

Watching him through narrowed eyes, she had a thought. It would really be interesting to see if the self-contained Aquarius man could be tempted beyond control.

Don't be foolish.

Yes, but wouldn't it be interesting. . . .

Chapter Two

"Did you two have a nice chat?" Carol inquired when Brittney joined her at the patio table.

"Yes."

"What did you talk about?"

"My future."

"Oh?"

"That's all," Brittney said. She picked up a cookie and sampled it. "Umm, Mrs. Muggs's cookies...delicious."

"What about your future?" Carol demanded, not at all distracted. She popped half a cookie into her mouth.

"He wanted to know if I was going for an advanced degree...such as the M.R.S." At the flicker of gleeful cunning in Carol's eyes, Brittney laughed. "Stop looking like a cat about to pounce. Actually, he wanted to apologize for his anger when we arrived. He's not interested in me."

"But you're interested in him."

"Well, even mere mortals can look at a god," she said with a cheerful grimace. "Not that it does any good."

"I knew it," Carol crowed. "You've had a thing for Daniel since that first summer you visited after our freshman year. Now we need to discuss strategy," she said in a lowered voice. "Daniel won't be easy."

"Like uncle, like niece." Brittney sighed. "You two love a challenge. Please don't give me any battle plans. I'm not going to war, so butt out, old friend."

"Phooey," Carol remarked. "I wonder what would be the best approach? Something subtle—"

"What are you two plotting?" Daniel closed his study door behind him and strolled across the patio. He selected a cookie and ate it in two bites, the same as Carol. Brittney liked to nibble and savor the taste of each and every crumb.

"I want to call up some people, see who's here for the summer. See you two later." Carol gave Brittney a conspiratorial glance and went into the house.

Just what she needed, Brittney groaned silently—Carol's obvious maneuvering. Brittney glanced at Daniel as he downed another fresh gingersnap, his gaze on the lake. He rarely looked her way. A momentary anger seized her. She'd like to make him sit up and take notice.

"What poor fellows are you two after this year?" he inquired, pulling out a chair and settling into it. He had a towel draped loosely across his shoulders. "I remember those twins from two years ago. They didn't know what had hit them. They called for months trying to get your number at school."

Brittney didn't like his sardonic amusement at their expense. "Carol doesn't permit summer romances to infringe on her winter ones," she explained with mock gravity.

His glance was penetrating. "What about you?"

"I don't have many romances."

"Why not?"

She smiled. "Because of you."

The remark got the result she wanted. He was looking directly at her, his perusal as probing as a dentist's drill.

Should she tell him of the wild yearning she'd once had for him? Hardly. Raw emotion wasn't the way to attract a man like Daniel, who, with his cool reserve, would probably laugh at her. Just how did one go about enticing a rugged individual like him?

The answer came to her. Laughter. And challenge. She would use a light touch; a teasing, playful, catch-me-if-you-can dare to his masculinity.

With a start, she realized she was doing just what she'd refused to consider with Carol—she was working out a strategy.

"Very funny," he said, abruptly rising. He wasn't smiling. "I'd better change and get back to work. I still have three reports to go over before dinner."

Without giving herself time to consider, she flicked him a sideways glance full of flirtatious humor. "All work and no play, Daniel." She murmured the warning.

His expression changed subtly, showing both interest and wariness at the caressing purr in her voice. "So, what did you have in mind?" he asked, taking up the challenge at once.

It was almost too easy, she mused. It appeared that a man reacted instinctively when a woman threw down the velvet glove, so to speak.

"Midnight swims in the lake, riding with the top down in a flashy red convertible, hiking through the woods, picnicking in a secluded meadow." She batted her lashes at him.

He threw back his head and laughed.

Brittney gave him a disgusted look. "You could at least be a little smitten when a woman flirts outrageously with you."

"You look like a kitten with a piece of fuzz caught on your whiskers . . . uh, lashes."

"Thanks."

He turned her face to his. "What's this all about, Brittney? Are you trying out your wiles on me?"

Now was not the time to back down, although she was more than a little chagrined that he saw through her so quickly. "Perhaps."

"Because if you are—" a slow, sexy smile spread over his mouth "—I might be susceptible."

With that, he walked to the door and disappeared inside the house, leaving her to ponder just exactly what he meant by that last remark.

She was still trying to figure it out while she dressed for dinner. Daniel seemed to have a firm grasp of feminine human nature. Had he meant what he said? Was he susceptible to her?

She leaned closer to the mirror. Her hazel-green eyes were large, the lashes long with a natural upsweep. Sighing, she pulled her hair, which was dark brown, thick and wavy, to one side and fastened it with a comb clip so that it cascaded over one shoulder, the longest tendrils lying over her breast.

From downstairs came the sound of a chime, then the striking of the clock. Seven. Time to meet in the library. She pulled on white pumps and left the room.

Carol surprised Brittney by being on time. They met in the hall and walked down the steps together, Carol in summery blue silk, Brittney in a white skirt and a golden silk blouse.

"Drinks?" Daniel asked when they entered the library.

"Tonic water for me," Carol said.

"Me, too," Brittney echoed. She didn't quite meet Daniel's eyes, but she was aware of his swift perusal.

Carol's mother stood by the window. She turned with a smile to greet the younger women. Brittney noticed the lines of strain around her eyes when Mrs. Montclair stepped forward.

"Hi, Mums," Carol said, bounding across the Oriental carpet to give her mother a smacking kiss and a bear hug.

Brittney was always amazed at Mrs. Montclair's tolerance. Her own mother would have moved away with a pained smile. "Please, Brittney, don't pounce and squeeze the life out of a person," she would have reprimanded.

"Hello, dear." Mrs. Montclair returned her daughter's kiss, then turned to their guest. "It's lovely to see you again, Brittney. I'm delighted that you'll be visiting with us."

"Perhaps we can persuade her to stay," Daniel cut in. He handed a glass to Carol, another to Brittney. "She says she's going to look for an apartment."

"Whatever for? We have plenty of room here," Mrs. Montclair said. "I'm sure Carol would be delighted if you stayed with us. I know I would."

"I've tried to talk sense into her, but she's just like Daniel when she makes up her mind," Carol complained.

"How's that?" Daniel inquired.

"Stubborn."

He gave Carol a mock-threatening glance, then turned to Brittney. "I'd like for you to stay, too. You're a good influence on my troublesome niece. Sometimes." His glance was speculative as he waited for her answer.

Brittney realized she had started something with her actions of the afternoon. Daniel wasn't going to let her wiggle out of the challenge she had impulsively issued. She realized she would have to continue as she had begun or else he'd think her a coward who couldn't face the consequences of her own acts.

Returning his gaze boldly, she murmured, "I'll think about it." Then she looked down demurely, knowing her eyes were her best feature. She'd use them to advantage.

Muggs peered around the door and nodded. Mrs. Montclair said their dinner was ready. Brittney felt a warm hand take her arm.

"Shall we?" Daniel asked.

Again she gave him a provocative glance from the corner of her eye. "Yes."

He looked at her without smiling. Tension arced between them. With an effort, she held his gaze.

He tightened his grip on her arm, then turned her toward the dining room, his expression closed.

Carol sat across from Brittney at the table and gave her a keen appraisal. All kinds of questions danced in her eyes, which were blue like Daniel's. Carol had her mother's blond hair, though, instead of the dark hair of the Montclairs.

Brittney wondered what had brought on that line of thought, then realized she was thinking of children. Her and Daniel's would have dark hair, but would their eyes be blue or hazel?

Her body warmed as she considered their children...and how they would be conceived. Making love with Daniel . . .

"What are you thinking?" Carol demanded. "Your face is glowing."

"Exactly what I was wondering," Daniel chimed in.

Brittney felt the heat increase, but she managed to laugh. "Maybe someday I'll tell you."

"That's two items you owe me," he said. "You were laughing to yourself at the lake earlier. You said you'd tell me about that someday, too."

She tilted her head and gave him a coy glance. "Someday I will." She hoped her soft laughter was mysterious and not just silly, which was how she felt.

Muggs diverted the conversation by serving a cool cucumber-and-radish salad. The vegetables had been grated and lightly coated with a sour-cream dressing. Grateful to have something else to concentrate on, Brittney took a bite. She could detect a bit of hot mustard and Parmesan cheese in the dressing.

"This is delicious, Beatrice," Daniel complimented his sister-in-law. "Is this another of your original recipes?"

Mrs. Montclair said that it was. Brittney realized that the older woman was quite good at managing the house. She knew Daniel entertained lavishly twice a year at the lakeside mansion: once at Christmas, when he threw a big party complete with weekend guests, ice-skating and tobogganing, as well as a formal dance; then, over the Fourth of July, he had a party for the "younger crowd"—a huge barbecue followed by dancing to a local pop band.

The rest of the year, he entertained in the city, living in his bachelor penthouse and taking...clients...? friends...? lovers...out to dine at the pricey restaurants. Jealousy reared its ugly head, and Brittney ground her teeth together.

Only people who were insecure were jealous, she reprimanded herself. Or desperately in love.

Well, she certainly wasn't the latter. She glanced up to find Daniel studying her. He had finished his salad and was holding his wineglass cupped between both hands. The soft light shone through the liquid so that it looked as if he held a pure crystal of some radiant gem.

My heart, she thought. He might as well be holding my heart.

"Daniel," Mrs. Montclair said. She sounded hesitant. Brittney noticed the lines of strain had deepened around her eyes. "I think I'd like to move to Arizona."

There was a surprised hush around the table.

"When did you decide that?" he asked.

"Well, I haven't decided. I'm considering." She laid her fork down and patted her mouth with her napkin. "You know my friend Joannie Caplan moved there last year. She writes of the climate in glowing terms. It would be warmer than here." A defensive note crept into her voice.

Brittney realized Mrs. Montclair was lonely. The woman had been a widow for several years; her daughter was grown and no longer needed mothering. Further, Daniel didn't really need her, either. He could arrange his own life without help.

"What about all the organizations you run?" Daniel asked, his tone teasing. "Could they survive?"

"They need someone younger to take over."

He frowned slightly. "You're only forty-five, Beatrice. I can't see you joining the rocking-chair brigade yet."

Mrs. Montclair's laughter held a nervous edge. "Well, I do get a twinge of arthritis when the winter wind blows, Daniel."

She needs to be needed, Brittney thought. She needs someone to care for; someone who cares about her in the special way between a man and a woman.

Don't we all?

"I see," he said slowly.

Brittney could tell he was already mulling things over in his mind, seeking a solution. How like him. Give him a problem, and he didn't rest until he found an answer. Daniel was the type who could hold a thousand details in his mind and never lose one.

"You could live in one of those posh resorts, Mums. You know the ones—where they have all those gorgeous golf and tennis pros to improve your game. Maybe you'd find someone and get married again. Of course, he'd have to sign an agreement to double my clothing allowance."

Carol looked at Daniel to see if this statement had had any effect on him. It hadn't.

"Behave yourself, Carol," Mrs. Montclair scolded. A slight blush highlighted her cheeks.

The conversation turned to clothes as Carol bemoaned the fact that she hadn't a thing to wear. "Brittney and I need to go over to the resort and check out the boutiques."

"Check out the young men," her mother corrected.

"That was the second thing on our list," Carol replied.

Daniel's head jerked up and he glared at her.

"What do you think?" Carol asked, pirouetting in front of an alcove formed by three mirrors.

Brittney looked up from the shorts she was considering. "You look great."

The dress was a halter sundress, white with blue dots. Rows of lace were sewn on the bodice. With little makeup and her hair gathered in a clasp on top of her head, Carol looked like a fresh-scrubbed prom queen in it.

"Maybe a little young," Brittney added.

"Yeah. I look like Little Bo-peep." She changed back to her shorts and blue knit top. "Come on. You can buy me lunch instead of the doughnut you owe me."

Brittney protested the increased cost all the way to the patio dining area. Carol ignored her. In a few minutes they were seated at a white table with a pink-and-white-striped umbrella.

The resort looked like a birthday cake with icing, Brittney decided, eyeing the building. The outside was painted pale salmon pink. The wood trim—Victorian ginger-bread—was stark white. The theme was carried out inside with pale pink and Mediterranean blue. Potted plants lined the walls and hung from the ceiling.

She pushed her sunglasses higher on her nose and surveyed the people at the surrounding tables. "There's a handsome specimen," she told Carol. "You'd better snap him up."

"Where?" Carol glanced around at the other early arrivals.

"The blond Adonis with the older man... Why, I know him—"

"The Adonis?" Carol looked eager.

"No, the older man. That's Mr. Sanders. Remember, he gave a zillion dollars to the college, and the dean was showing him around the campus? I was introduced in British Lit."

"Let's go get reacquainted," Carol suggested with a lazy drawl and a half smile. She stood.

"Poor Adonis, he hasn't a chance," Brittney murmured, knowing that look on her friend's face. Perhaps she should go after her goal with the same open determination.

The funny thing was, when Daniel wasn't around, she was positive she could do it; when he appeared, she wasn't so sure. Her emotional balance became precarious. She had to learn to be as cool as he was and as blatant as Carol. She got up and followed her friend.

Carol gave her an expectant glance when they neared the table where the two men studied the menu. Brittney cleared her throat. "Hello, Mr. Sanders," she said brightly, hand extended. "I'm Brittney Chapel. I met you on campus earlier this spring. Your endowment was a great help to the department."

The man and his companion stood. "Why, thank you, uh, Miss Chapel. It's a pleasure to meet you again." They shook hands. "This is my nephew, Harry."

The Adonis shook hands with her. He really was something to behold—golden blond hair, soulful blue eyes, clean-cut features, an all-American physique.

"Please, call me Brittney. I'd like you to meet my friend, Carol." She'd let Carol elaborate on her family if she wanted.

Carol smiled her knock-'em-dead smile while she shook hands with both men. "Brittney and I are school chums," she explained, "recently graduated and out to make our fortunes."

They were asked to join the gentlemen, which they promptly did, due to Carol's quick acceptance of the invitation. Brittney smothered a laugh. In ten minutes flat, Carol would have both men eating out of her hand.

"And how do you intend to make this fortune you mentioned?" Harry asked, already dazzled by Carol.

"Well, Brittney's going to work at the museum in town. I thought I'd find a rich husband." She turned to the uncle. "Just how large was that endowment?"

That brought another laugh. From that moment, they were at ease with one another and proceeded to have an entertaining lunch.

Daniel reread the paragraph, then realized he'd already read it three times. With about as much comprehension as the first two tries, he admitted, disgusted by his lack of control. It wasn't like him to let his mind wander.

Lord, but he was tired of the details of life. Of paperwork, he admitted. He wished he were in the north, filling his lungs with pine-scented air, doing the kind of work that put a man to sleep at night.

The man-woman thing again. It was a strong distraction from business. Brittney filled his thoughts.

Sitting close to her on the raft yesterday had produced the same sparks of interest that he'd felt when he'd first met her.

She'd flirted with him, deliberately and provocatively. Was she playing a game, casting him in the role of the older, worldly male and trying out her feminine skills on him?

He didn't know her level of experience, but he knew she felt the same attraction he did. If she challenged him again the way she had the day before, she might get more than she bargained for.

He heaved a deep breath. She was a temptation he wasn't sure he could resist anymore. Since the time she'd fallen off the Hobie Cat and he'd hauled her back aboard, dripping wet and absolutely gorgeous, he'd been aware of her.

Aware? Come on, let's get truthful. More like sizzling. Every time he was around her, he felt as if he had caught a fever.

Surely she was old enough to know what she was doing. She was... what? Twenty-one, close to twenty-two. Yeah, old enough, his libido insisted, while his conscience hesitated.

His body reacted with the pure logic of desire: he was attracted to her. She apparently felt the same. They were adults; so what was the problem?

He tossed the papers onto his desk, careless of the contract that meant several millions of dollars to the company. The house was too quiet.

Brittney and Carol had gone to the resort to shop. Beatrice was getting her hair done. Perhaps he'd join his niece and her friend at lunch. His smile was sardonic.

Much to his disgust, he'd come to the house every blasted time he knew she was due to arrive with Carol. One look and he backed off, knowing he wanted too much—more than he felt she had been willing to give in the past.

But now? an internal voice questioned.

He had to admit he didn't know. It was a new sensation. Brittney excited him in a way no woman ever had. She had a quiet, congenial exterior, but what was she like inside? He sensed depths of unplumbed passion....

Suddenly restless again, he felt the need to break free, to shake off restraints and live life his own way.

Standing, he stretched and yawned. His sleep had been disturbed last night. He kept remembering Brittney's suggestion of a midnight swim in the lake. He'd prowled the house for hours, haunted, unable to settle in the library and get on with business.

Truthfully, he'd half expected her to appear. Or maybe he'd only hoped she would.

Forget it, he advised, assessing the situation coolly. He wasn't a kid just out of school. He shouldn't tangle with one who was trying her wings, probably for the first time.

Good advice. He'd follow it.

Having sorted this out, he decided he'd go down to the resort and treat the kids to lunch. He needed to relax. He would read the contract later... and think about Beatrice's sudden desire to move to Arizona. She seemed dissatisfied with life. Maybe he should suggest she get a job.

Once he'd thought to be a great archaeologist. A boy's dreams. Now he had a man's work to do, running the various companies the family owned—logging and milling, papermaking and printing. His responsibilities were well-ordered and logical.

Too bad women weren't that way. Mostly, they were just another chore to take care of. Beatrice wanted him to make all her decisions, just as she'd forced his brother to do when Adam was alive.

Love was the ultimate demand. From observation and a couple of close calls, he had determined that women wanted a man's heart, his body, his soul and, for good measure, his wallet and his every thought. He wasn't inclined to share that much of himself.

He strode out of the room, his tennis shoes flashing white in the noonday sun as he walked the short distance along the narrow road to the resort. He found the girls on the patio.

Irritation heated his blood when he saw them laughing with two men at the table. Trust his niece to pick up two strangers right off.

Brittney seemed to be enjoying herself, too. He noticed the smooth line of her throat when she shook back her hair and laughed at something the older man was saying. Lord, the guy was old enough to be her father! Fury welled in him.

He saw her turn her head and catch a glimpse of him. Her laughter faded as she met his gaze for a split second, then she smiled as if she were delighted to see him. For Daniel it was like stepping out of the dark into the sun. He strolled over to join the laughing couples.

"Darn, too late," he said with mock regret while approaching the table. "I thought I'd treat you gals to lunch, but I waited too long, I see."

Mr. Sanders—he'd asked Carol and Brittney to call him Hank—stood and introduced himself. Daniel noticed who the other man was, the one who seemed taken with Carol, at the same time the fellow recognized Daniel.

"Montclair," Harry said in surprise. "You know Carol and Brittney?"

Daniel felt the fury rising again. "Carol's my niece."

"Have you two met?" Carol asked.

Daniel nodded. "Montclair Printing will be doing several jobs for Sanders Catalogs."

"I was at your place yesterday," Harry explained to Carol, "going over the contracts with Montclair and his attorney. Uncle Hank, this is the head of Montclair products. We got a darned good price from them."

Daniel was aware of Brittney scrutinizing him. Her gaze was wary. He relaxed, letting the unexpected anger cool. He should have known they wouldn't lack masculine company; Carol and Brittney had always attracted men in droves.

He curbed his inclination to be rude. The Sanders company compiled directories—city, business, product and telephone directories—and was well-known all over the United States. The contract was a lucrative one.

"We're doing the buffet today," Carol told him. "Get a salad and join us. We'll wait for you."

"All right." He quickly selected vegetables from the huge salad barge, which was actually a rowboat filled with ice and bowls of crisp greens and sliced vegetables, and returned to the table, squeezing in between Carol and Brittney.

The conversation was mostly between the nephew, Harry, and Carol, he noted. They seemed to have an equal amount of quips and witty repartee and enjoyed sparring with each other.

"I waited last night," he said in a quiet aside to Brittney, forgetting his intentions to treat her as merely a young friend of his niece.

She lifted those incredible lashes and gave him a candid glance from eyes that were green with a touch of dark gold and gray. "Waited?"

"For the midnight swim," he reminded her.

A flush added a delicate hue to her pale skin. Although her hair was dark, her skin tended to be fair. A picture of what she looked like all over suddenly leaped into his mind with the force of an exploding mine. He sucked in a deep breath. Careful, he cautioned, or this attraction could get out of hand.

"I thought you might be too tired from your business meeting," she murmured. She gave him an oblique glance, provocative and filled with the ancient knowledge of women.

His instincts were aroused now, and he could feel hunger stirring, the excitement of the chase beginning. He just wasn't sure if he was the hunter or the hunted.

He gazed at Brittney. There was only one thing to do, he decided. Stick around and find out.

Brittney was aware of Daniel with every cell on the right side of her body. Sometimes he brushed her arm when he leaned forward to take a bite of salad. Each time they touched, she felt a thrill.

Whenever she met his eyes, she saw the intense interest of a man for a woman. So she had caught his attention with her teasing remarks yesterday. Well, she had started the game, now she had to carry through.

"Tonight?" she invited, her voice husky, not by deliberation, but due to some natural chemistry when he was near.

"You're on," he whispered.

His breath ruffled the hair at her temple, sending chills up her arm. She rubbed them. Across the table, Mr. Sanders watched with an amused expression in his eyes. He was a nice person, she thought. A gentleman of breeding. And close to Beatrice in age....

"Why don't you invite Mr. Sanders and his nephew to dinner?" she asked Daniel, leaning close to him. This time her action was planned. She brushed his hair with her lips as she spoke.

His eyes narrowed. For a second, she thought he was angry again, as he'd been when he'd first approached them, but she was mistaken. Now he was smiling affably and agreeing to the idea. When there was a break in the conversation, he issued the invitation to both men.

"Oh, what a good idea, Daniel." Carol beamed at him. Her summer romance was off to a good start.

Brittney only half listened as the other two briefly consulted and added the dinner to their plans.

"Will you join us here afterward for the guest show? We promised to participate," Mr. Sanders explained.

Brittney was amazed. She couldn't picture him or Harry acting in one of those guest skits the resorts loved to press people into doing. She thought of the acts as some kind of macabre punishment visited on the vacationers by the resort's social director.

"What are you going to do?" Carol demanded, her blue eyes clearly showing her surprise.

Harry grinned. "You'll have to wait and see."

Neither he nor his uncle would tell, no matter how Carol tried to cajole the information out of them. At last the trio stood and said their goodbyes.

"Seven o'clock, then," Daniel said, reminding the men of the dinner hour. They promised to be there.

"Well," Carol said with relish as she, Brittney and Daniel walked along the road, "this summer certainly has great promise."

Daniel linked his hands with hers and Brittney's. "Yes, I'd say it seems to be shaping up that way."

Brittney's hand tingled as he tightened his hold. If she joined him tonight for a swim, they'd kiss. She knew that as surely as she knew the moon would be in its last quarter. And if they kissed—she closed her eyes for a painful second—if they kissed, what then?

When she sighed and gazed once more at the lake, Daniel leaned close. "Were you thinking of tonight?"

She nodded. That was the second time in two days he'd read her like a typewritten report.

"Are you going to renege?" he asked.

Brittney shook her head. "Are you?"

A sudden premonition chilled him to the bone. He could be getting in deeper than he intended. He shook off the warning. "I wouldn't miss it for the world," he said.

"What are you two whispering about?" Carol demanded.

"Frankly, my dear, none of your business," he replied equably.

Carol made a rude face at him. "You'll get your comeuppance one of these days, Daniel, and I'll be there to laugh."

He followed them into the house and up the stairs. He had a bedroom suite down the hall from their rooms.

Brittney had no sooner closed her door than Carol knocked on the interconnecting one and entered without waiting for an answer. She had a book in her hand.

"I thought you might be interested in how your and Daniel's signs meshed," she proclaimed, flopping onto the bed after bunching a pillow against the headboard.

"Actually, I'm not."

Carol ignored her. "Daniel's birthday is January 22nd. Aquarius is the fixed-air sign. That means his personality can't be changed. I wanted to warn you—"

"Everyone can grow and change," Brittney said with conviction.

"He's as dependable as a security blanket, but he might tend to be rigid," she intoned, reading from the book. She looked up. "This type doesn't act on impulse, so don't expect flowers except on your birthday."

"But Aquarians are ruled by Uranus," Brittney reminded her friend. "If you can get past the reserve, there's a core of passion and devotion—"

"You've been reading astrology!"

Brittney looked as if she'd been caught in a criminal act. "Well, no...that is, I did glance through a book one day."

Carol flipped over a few pages. "You're Sagittarius. A fire sign. Aha! Air feeds fire. Now, what does that mean?" She studied Brittney. "Daniel will feed you—"

"I don't want to be fed by Daniel. It makes me sound like a parasite, like that love vine that twines itself over a bush until it smothers it. Daniel wouldn't like that."

"True."

Brittney grinned. "Give up on the stars and get out of here. I'm going to take a nap."

Carol bounced off the bed. "Something keeping you awake at night? His room is just three doors down the hall." She dashed out of the room just as a pillow hit the door.

Brittney retrieved the weapon and tossed it back on the bed. She lay down and closed her eyes, but her brain refused to switch off. The telephone interrupted her count of sheep.

"Call for you on line one," Muggs said.

"Thanks." She pushed the button and answered.

"Brittney?"

She recognized the cultured voice with the faint Southern edge. "Hello, Mother. How are you?"

"Fine. Are you settled in?"

The niceties first, then down to business. "Yes, I am."

"That's good. Is the weather pleasant?"

Her mother's voice was more cordial than usual. Brittney couldn't prevent the wariness that infused her. "The weather is perfect for lounging by the lake. Unfortunately, I've got to look for a place to live on Monday."

"You could probably stay with Carol, couldn't you?"

Her mother wasn't really interested. Brittney wished she'd say what she wanted and get it over with. "Yes, but it's better that I establish my own place. How's Sonny?"

"That's what I wanted to speak to you about—"

"I can't send him any more of my allowance," Brittney quickly cut in. "I only have enough money to get me through—"

"Naturally, I wouldn't expect you to run short," her mother said, her voice going cold. "I thought you might approach your grandfather. After all, your father left you a large legacy."

Brittney ignored the sharp hurt the request quickly produced. Sonny was the child of her mother's first marriage. Once she'd heard her mother tell a close friend that "there's never a love like the first love." That had been Sonny's father. Her own father had provided security for a young widow with a small child. She knew her mother couldn't help loving that first child more. After all, he had been born of love, not of the necessity to produce an heir.

"Grandfather isn't well. I'd rather not disturb him."

In truth, her grandfather had told her not to intervene for Sonny again. He had no respect for a man who couldn't live on his own income. Sonny had worked as a manager in her grandfather's oil-distribution company for four years, but his tastes were those of a king.

Caught between her mother and grandfather was like being squeezed between the proverbial rock and a hard place. Neither liked the other. They used her as an intermediary.

Brittney knew her half brother was envious of the fact that her father had come from a wealthy family and that she would someday inherit Stony River, the plantation outside of Shreveport, as well as a large fortune. However, she still had to live on a very frugal allowance—one that would probably stop as soon as she was settled in her job. Her grandfather didn't coddle people.

"Surely you need money to furnish an apartment."

Brittney understood what her mother was suggesting. "I can't lie, Mother. My furniture from college and from my old room at Stony River will be shipped to me."

"I hope you never need anything from your brother," Mrs. Chapel said coolly. "He might remember these little slights."

"I'm sorry," Brittney said. "I just don't have the money."

Her mother abruptly changed the subject. They chatted for another minute, then said goodbye.

Brittney realized she was trembling when she hung up. She always felt so guilty after talking to her mother, as if she had failed her yet again. Still, there was nothing she could do. She hadn't lied about that.

She put her arm over her eyes, blocking out the light from the window, and wondered what her mother must have been like in her younger days, before she'd developed that cool edge of reserve. Surely she had been warmer, more outgoing, before the loss of her first love had changed her forever.

Brittney fought against a sense of doom. Daniel had been her first love. But perhaps what she had felt for him was a girl's idealistic version of love.

Her vision blurred. It was entirely too possible that that first dazzling love would be forever enshrined in her heart as the best, just as her mother's first love seemed to be.

Chapter Three

Brittney dithered in front of the closet. She had never been a ditherer, but then, she'd never tried to tempt a man like Daniel before, either.

The guest skits at the resort were usually casual affairs. Slacks, she thought. A gleam came into her eyes. She pulled out a crepe silk blouse of deep teal green and a pair of harem-cut black slacks. Black high-heeled sandals. Gold, dangly earrings. Three gold chains of varying lengths nestled between her breasts. She surveyed herself in the mirror: casual chic.

The chime sounded seven. The doorbell rang at the same instant. She went downstairs.

Daniel was pouring drinks for the two men when she paused in the hall just outside the doorway to the library. Beatrice and Carol were nowhere in sight.

"Brittney, come in," Daniel invited. "What would you like tonight? I have a chilled bottle of white wine."

"That would be fine," she said. "Hello, Harry. Mr. Sanders."

"Hank, please." The older man took her hand, holding it in one of his and patting it with the other. "You look lovely."

"Thank you."

When she took the wine from Daniel, she glanced into his eyes. It was like running into a solid wall. The warmth of his greeting had been replaced by fury.

Startled, she turned away.

"Harry, do you like to canoe?" she asked to cover her retreat. "Carol loves to explore the lake."

"Really? The hotel has canoes for rent. Perhaps I'll ask her out tomorrow."

He was pathetically eager. Brittney felt sorry for him and hoped he wasn't going to get his heart bruised when Carol went off to Europe or the Caribbean or wherever her next impulse took her. "I like it, too."

"You must join us," he said at once.

A gentleman. She shook her head. "I'll rent my own."

"Then you must let me paddle it for you," Mr. Sanders said.

She peeked at Daniel. He was staring into his glass.

"What are you guys planning?" Carol demanded, walking into the room with her long, elegant stride.

She was dressed in a gold silk trouser outfit that caressed her graceful limbs with each movement. Her hair was styled on top of her head, but curls strayed enticingly around her neck. Harry stepped forward to meet her. Too easy, Brittney thought. Carol needed more of a challenge.

"A striking couple," Mr. Sanders murmured, a worried look in his eyes.

"Very," Brittney agreed, meeting the older man's gaze. They exchanged a glance of understanding: she would warn

Carol about hurting other people; he would warn his nephew about taking a summer romance too seriously. They smiled at each other.

Turning, she ran into Daniel's stone-wall perusal. What was he thinking that turned his thoughts so dark?

Harry explained to Carol about the canoe trip. She thought it sounded like a lark. "Let's take a picnic lunch and see how many kinds of ducks we can identify. There're usually coots and loons. And mallards, of course." She gave Harry an appraising glance from his shining blond hair to his polished dress shoes.

"That sounds like fun," Daniel cut in, surprising the two young women. "Perhaps I'll join you."

Carol raised her brows at Brittney and gave her a pointed look. Brittney shrugged. She had no idea what he was thinking.

Footsteps sounded in the hall. Mrs. Montclair entered the library. Like her daughter, she had a flair for clothes. Her long dress was a brilliant silk print of white on blue. It brought out the color of her eyes.

"My sister-in-law. Beatrice, Hank Sanders and his nephew, Harry." Daniel made the introductions.

Beatrice was a skilled hostess, Brittney noted. The woman soon knew that both Hank and Harry were named Harold after a favorite grandfather. "Possibly because he was the one with the money," Mr. Sanders said with a twinkle in his gray eyes.

"I'm sure he was delighted to have two handsome namesakes."

Brittney watched Mrs. Montclair charm the older man just as Carol had charmed the younger one. She decided she was going to have to take a lesson from their books and be more aggressive toward Daniel. She glanced his way to find him watching her, his gaze moody with some emotion she couldn't decipher.

"Dinner is ready. Shall we go in, Mr. Sanders?" Mrs. Montclair smiled at their guest.

"Hank," he said. "Please."

"Hank," she repeated, looking up at him, her eyes bluer than a summer sky, her gaze just as warm.

He held out his arm, and she slipped her hand into the crook of his elbow. They walked out together. Harry quirked a brow, grinned, then executed a crisp bow and did the same to Carol. They left the library.

Daniel looked amused. "Looks like it's just you and me, babe," he intoned.

Brittney was taken aback by his mood changes, from warmth to anger to teasing, all in the space of thirty minutes. Trying to return his levity, she asked, "So, should we split?"

"Let's go eat," he said dryly, holding out his arm.

She tucked her hand into the curve of his arm, liking the warmth she found there. He was dressed in a dark gray suit with a blue and gray tie and looked wealthy and successful. His sudden jocularity disconcerted her. It was as if he had retreated behind a wall of good-natured humor.

Without warning, he lifted her hand to his lips and kissed her fingertips. When he resettled it on his arm, she caught a glimpse of the fiery center she had wanted to explore, and trembled with uncertainty.

Was she woman enough to handle Daniel's passion? He was air, he could produce lightning, and she was tinder, ready to kindle at his touch.

He seated her at his right. Carol was at his left, with Harry beside her. Mr. Sanders was between Brittney and Mrs. Montclair.

The dinner was a gay affair. The conversation never lagged, although Brittney added little to it. Daniel, she noted, participated well. When the men discussed the current economic climate, his opinions were concise and clear.

When the meal was over, the two guests reminded them of the evening's entertainment at the resort.

Brittney fetched a lacy black shawl from her room in case the wind was cool off the lake. When she returned downstairs, Daniel was waiting for her by the front door. The others had strolled on. It was natural that she was paired with Daniel. It felt right. Did he notice?

The night was so beautiful, it made her want to recite poems. Fireflies flickered in the meadow, and the moon gleamed like a silver lantern, showering the lake with silver. The walk down the lane was much too short.

The three couples found seats at one of the tables. The umbrellas had been removed so everyone could see the stage. The first act was a comedy routine with a professional juggler and a guest as his helper. They did well together, garnering several laughs during their performance.

Slightly more than an hour later, the last act was announced. Harry and his uncle went to the stage where they were joined by two other men. They hummed a note in harmony, then began to sing, "Down by the old—not the new, but the old—mill stream . . ."

Mrs. Montclair laughed in delight. "A barbershop quartet!" she exclaimed.

The group was surprisingly good. They ended by singing "Row, Row, Row Your Boat" in parts. Later, walking beside Daniel in the shadows of the maple trees, the final words repeated over and over in her mind: "Life is but a dream."

But dreams could be so sweet, she mused, drifting along in a romantic fantasy. Life could, too. With the proper person.

Harry and Hank stayed for a nightcap. Daniel said he had work to do and excused himself. Not wanting to be the fifth wheel, Brittney said good-night and went to her room. She dressed for bed and sat in a chair by the window, looking out at the stars. It was after midnight before she heard Carol and her mother come upstairs. A few minutes later, the house was entirely quiet.

She could hear the heavy beat of her heart as blood coursed sluggishly through her veins. A lethargy enveloped her. She could hardly move, her limbs were so heavy.

Her room was at the side of the house, her view of the lake limited. She couldn't see the boathouse pier from her window. For a long time, she sat very still. Then, in the total silence, she slipped out of her nightgown and into a bathing suit.

She made no conscious decision, but followed an instinct as old as womankind. She went down the steps and out the side door.

The lawn was damp, chilling her feet. She walked onto the pier and out to the end. She was alone.

Somewhere on the lake, a duck fluttered and fussed at its mate, then quieted. The moon was already disappearing behind the trees. Out on the raft, something moved.

Her heart leaped.

Daniel.

Without hesitation, she dived into the water. The sensation of cold lasted only a second. She swam with hardly a ripple through the inky liquid, which felt like something magic caressing her skin as she moved. When she reached the raft, strong hands were there to lift her up.

"I wondered if you'd come," Daniel said. His smile flashed in the dark, then was gone. He released her.

"Yes." She felt breathless, urgent, on edge.

She wanted so many things—to feel his arms around her, holding her closer and closer, his body trembling as hers was. She wanted to touch him, make love to him with all the unleashed passion of her fiery nature.

Fiery nature?

How did she know she possessed such a thing? She wasn't sure, but it seemed a part of herself that she should guard. He was here because she had intrigued him with her playful challenge. She had to keep on the same way she had started.

Lifting her chin, she shook back her wet hair and let the pale light play over her shoulders and throat. "Why did you come?"

"Curiosity," he replied without hesitation.

She laughed huskily. "The same curiosity that killed the cat?"

"I don't intend to get that close." His smile flashed briefly in the dark. He was distant again, using the sharp edge of humor to turn the conversation his way.

She wasn't having it.

"I think you do." She stepped an inch closer. "I think you came out here to get very much closer. When are you going to kiss me, Daniel?" She was amazed at her boldness.

He clasped the hand she laid on his chest. "Sure of yourself, aren't you?"

If he touched her, he would know she was lying. Tremors ran over her skin like fire. "Of what I want, yes."

"Perhaps I was just testing you, wanting to see how far you would go...if you showed up."

She had been wondering the very same thing. "I'm here, so why don't we find out?"

Daniel released her hand and placed his hands at her waist. He liked touching her there. Between the gently curving hardness of her ribs and pelvis, her narrow waist was soft and tantalizing, reminding him of other places that would be as soft, as yielding.

He felt her body tremble.

"Are you afraid of me, Brittney?" He heard the hoarseness of desire in his voice. He throbbed with a heat that the cold lake water could not cool.

"No."

He frowned at the quick denial, which was accompanied by another slight tremor. He pulled her against him and massaged roughly along her spine. He kissed the hair at her temple.

With a grace he was sure she wasn't aware of, she curled against him, seeking his warmth, sending fire to all parts of his body. He'd never needed a woman so much that he ached with it. She'd have to be numb not to feel what she did to him.

Warnings rang through the haze of his desire. This was simply a summer romance. They both understood that, didn't they? He'd better make sure. "I don't want to hurt you."

"Why would you?" she countered.

"You know what I mean," he said, his tone harsher.

She leaned against his enclosing embrace. "Are you asking if you're my first lover?"

That hadn't been his meaning at all. Something akin to shock ran through him, followed immediately by other emotions that he hadn't had time to analyze.

"Am I?"

Brittney recognized the sound of anger in the question. Wary, she thought of lying, but was afraid of the consequences when he discovered the truth. Instinctively she knew better than to try that tactic with Daniel.

"Am I?" he demanded again. He slid his hands along her back and grasped her shoulders, moving her from his hard warmth.

"Yes."

The whispered word echoed in the dark, baldly, starkly vibrating between them.

He muttered an expletive that singed her ears. "I'm not one of your college dates," he informed her. "When a woman comes on to me the way you've done since you arrived, I don't usually stop to ask questions. I assume she knows what she's doing."

"I do," Brittney protested. She laid her hands flat on his chest. Intrigued, she stroked the crisply curling hairs, loving the sensual caress against her palms.

"Like hell." He grabbed her wrists and folded her arms behind her back. "I've watched you and Carol play your games for three years, driving those young pups crazy over you, then laughing when you left them. If you think I'll let you use me like that and just walk away, think again."

She let herself curve into him. The heavy strength of his body was unmistakable. He might be angry, but he wanted her. A small thrill ran through her. "I want you," she said, pressing her face into his neck.

He went very still.

She kissed along his collarbone, found the hollow at his throat, followed the rigid cord in his neck to his jaw. Reaching, she kissed his cheek, the corner of his mouth—

His body pulsed against her as only the thin material of their swimsuits separated them.

He lifted his head then, and she couldn't touch his mouth. She was disappointed. She resumed her caresses along his jaw.

"Daniel—"

"Dammit," he said, "you're playing with fire."

"You're air. I'm fire," she corrected. "Love me, Daniel. I've wanted you for so long."

She felt his breath against her face as the air rushed out of his lungs at her plea. "My God, you'd tempt a man to forget every grain of sense he had."

The world spun as he lifted her, then laid her down. She felt the spongy texture of the mat under her shoulders and thighs and the crisp texture of Daniel's legs and chest along the front length of her body as he partially covered her.

She discovered her arms were free. She wrapped them around his shoulders. The moon had set behind the trees, and they were concealed by the darkness. Longing drove all thoughts away.

"Is this what you want?" he asked, nuzzling hungrily against her throat. "A coupling in the dark with no promises given, no ties, no thoughts of tomorrow?"

She didn't answer.

"What if you get pregnant?" he continued ruthlessly, his lips grazing hers, taunting but not fulfilling.

"I won't. When I got the museum position, I started . . ."

He raised himself off her. "So you were planning this all along," he said slowly. "The seduction of Daniel." He laughed without humor. "And to think I was worried about your innocence."

She didn't know what to say. Behind the cynical words was something else. Hurt? Disappointment?

Or was she imagining things?

"I'm physically innocent, but I'm not naive, Daniel. I know about men and women." She caressed his shoulders with skimming, butterfly touches. "I've wanted you for three years. Surely you've known that."

"You were too young then—"

"And now?"

"I see you as a woman," he admitted. He rubbed her cheek with his fingertips, back and forth with a steady rhythm that drove her wild.

"Well?" she invited, smiling up at him. A beat of triumph went through her like a single pure note from a trumpet. Through the dark, she could detect the flash of his eyes, but saw no answering smile. He wasn't happy about wanting her.

It seemed to take forever, but his lips finally met hers. Their first kiss, she thought. She'd remember.

His lips were firm, warm, moist on hers. He caressed her mouth with a thousand different nuances of pressure and position. The kiss was endless.

With subtle expertise, he lightened the pressure. His tongue joined the sensual assault, teasing her lips apart, finding the inner sweetness. If she could have opened her eyes, she was sure the light surrounding their entwined bodies would be dazzling.

She felt his hand move along her side, massage the indentation of her waist. He moved farther, his fingers brushing the edge of her suit, then the sensitive skin of her leg. Again. Again.

Wildness gathered in her. She fought to retain control when she wanted to cry out in ecstasy, to pull him closer and closer. She held back the entreaty to finish what they had started that trembled on every quick-drawn breath she took.

A quick coupling in the dark, that was all this was. Wasn't that what he said? No ties, no promises of tomorrow? Wasn't that what she had decided she was willing to settle for—a summer of romance?

Before she had time to consider an answer, Daniel pulled away from her arms. He drew his knees up and dropped his head over his arms, his breathing ragged and harsh.

She sat up more slowly. Moving to him, she laid a hand on his shoulder. "Daniel?"

He raised his head. "You'd better be damned sure of where you're heading. This road is a one-way street, Brittney. There'll be no going back once we . . . travel it."

"I know."

With a lithe motion, he rose and stepped to the edge of the raft. He was a slim, powerfully built silhouette against the sky. With a spring, he dived into the lake. A few feet out, he turned on his back and waited for her.

Anger overcame the passion. He had closed himself off again. Sighing, she followed him into the fluid darkness of the water.

At the boathouse, he opened a locker, tossed her a towel and took one for himself. They dried off in silence. He walked with her into the house and up the steps to her door.

"Tomorrow," he said, "I want an answer from you about us. Do you understand?"

She shook her head. "You said you wouldn't let me laugh and walk away at the end of the summer. What did you mean?"

He ran a hand through his hair. "You and Carol play games. You think you can kiss and tease and go no further. That won't work with me. I'm a man, and I want more than kisses. Push me too far, and you'll find out how much more."

"I see."

He lifted her chin and stared into her eyes. A tiny nightlight provided the only illumination. "Be sure, Brittney. A man could become addicted to your kisses, but they're not enough."

He lowered his head until their mouths touched. Their tongues refused to be left out of the feast. The kiss lengthened. She felt the swelling of his body and sensed a response deep within him.

Dear God, how she wanted him.

When the kiss ended, they clung together, breathing heavily. "Yeah, you're fire," he whispered, caressing her neck under her damp hair. "You can send me up in a blaze with just a look."

She opened her mouth to ask him to stay with her. He laid a finger over her lips. "Tomorrow. Sleep on it. I have a feeling that once we start something, it isn't going to be easy to stop it." His smile had a certain whimsical quality she'd never seen.

With a gentle hand, he pushed her inside and closed the door after her. She glided across the room, still lost in the sensual haze of romance and passion. She showered and dressed once more in her nightgown. Once in bed, she couldn't sleep.

Daniel's advice ran through her mind. And his last words, spoken in a tone shaded with a light irony and resignation. Did that mean he was giving up on fighting their attraction? She decided it did. He had left the matter up to her.

A quiver of tingles rushed along her spine. There was no decision at all to make. She already knew the answer to the enigma of Daniel Montclair and Brittney Chapel.

Marriage. It was as simple as that.

She could hardly wait to see his face when she told him.

Chapter Four

Brittney woke with a start the next morning. She leaped out of bed as if the hounds of hell were after her, then remembered it was Sunday. Daniel would still be here.

Today she had to face him. A sort of "morning after."

She smiled. Her blood thrummed softly in anticipation. She hadn't changed her mind during the night. She'd only decided not to accept a summer romance.

After a quick wash, she slipped into white cotton slacks and a pink blouse with long, loose sleeves trimmed in white lace. She brushed her hair and applied pink gloss. After sliding her feet into scuffs, she went downstairs.

Just as she had expected, Daniel was the only one up. He was sitting at the table, reading the *New York Times*.

"Here, you want a section?" he asked, looking up when she came into the breakfast room. He had no smile of welcome for her. In fact, his gaze was downright hostile.

"I'll have something to eat first." Going to the sideboard, she mulled over his unfriendly attitude. She selected a bagel, cream cheese and hot tea, then returned to the table. Daniel stayed buried behind the paper.

Her blood began a slow boil. So he was back to ignoring her. He'd obviously had second thoughts about them.

Well, that was too bad. She hadn't changed her mind about wanting him. She slapped cream cheese over the bagel and bit into it angrily.

He continued to read.

Muggs came in and replenished Daniel's coffee. He removed the used dishes, checked the platters on the sideboard and left. Not a word was spoken.

Brittney became quietly furious. While she had learned to control the excesses of her other emotions, sometimes her temper got the better of her. She decided to leave before she said something she'd regret.

"Leaving?" Daniel inquired, peering over the paper. His expression was as flat as a two-dimensional drawing.

"No, just getting some more tea. I'd like the arts-and-leisure section, please."

She poured more hot water, dunked a tea bag viciously and returned to the table. He had laid the section she'd requested near her place. She sat down and started reading.

"Oh, by the way," she said, opening the paper to the second page, "I've decided what I want...and what I'm going to do."

"What?" he asked, sounding slightly bored from behind the sports news.

"I've decided I'm going to court you."

The silence was ominous.

The paper was lowered. His eyebrows arched; his eyes narrowed to icy blue slits. "Just what the hell does that mean?" he demanded.

This wasn't exactly the way she'd pictured the scene. But, she sighed internally, such was life. "Well, I thought I'd invite you on a few dates, lull you into complacency, then pop the question when you were least expecting it." She smiled brightly at him.

His scowl disappeared into a bland expression. "Marriage, Brittney? Is that what we're talking about?"

"Yes, Daniel, it is," she said with mock solemnity. She dropped her lashes over her eyes so he wouldn't see the gleam in their revealing depths.

"Forget it." He tossed the paper on the table and picked up his coffee cup. His eyes never left her.

"Why?"

"It wouldn't work, that's why."

"How do you know?" She made her voice soft, seductive; and gazed directly at him.

A muscle ticked once, twice, before his jaw hardened into stone. Oh, this was going to be fun, she thought to herself. After all this time of ignoring her, she was going to drive him insane. Her conscience niggled her, but she rationalized that he deserved this treatment.

"I just do," he snapped.

He ran a hand through his hair, revealing his inner turmoil. She smiled slightly. At least she was getting to him.

"Perhaps you haven't thought it out, Daniel—"

He stood abruptly. His chair made a screeching sound on the oak flooring. "Perhaps you haven't thought at all." He walked out without looking back. Down the hall, she heard the door to his study slam shut.

"—otherwise you'd see the advantages," she continued as if he were still present. Replacing the bagel on her plate, she went outside and let the sun warm her.

"Do you want to go canoeing with us?" Carol asked when she came down two hours later. "We're going to picnic at the far end of the lake."

"You and Harry?" Brittney laughed. "He'd probably throw me overboard if I barged in."

"No, he wouldn't. Harry's a gentleman." Carol was browsing through the Sunday paper as she made this statement.

Brittney remembered her unspoken promise to Harry's uncle last night. "Uh, Carol, about Harry..."

"Yes?"

Brittney recognized the don't-give-me-a-lecture tone. She suddenly felt sorry for Harry. No matter what she said to Carol, the man had already fallen hard. "Let him down gently, won't you? Unrequited love is a killer."

Carol relaxed and returned Brittney's smile. "I will." She crossed her heart. "Things not going well with my dear uncle?"

Brittney shrugged. "When I told him I was going to court him, he had an adverse reaction."

"You told him what!" Carol's eyes went wide, then she whooped with laughter.

"It wasn't all that funny," Brittney said with a wry twist to her mouth.

"I'm not laughing at you. It's Daniel. He's probably still running. That man is bachelor material, no doubt about it."

"Why?"

"Why?" Carol thought for a minute. "Well, he just is. I can't see him losing his head over anything, especially a woman." Her expression softened. "He's a fool not to grab you up. I'll tell him."

Brittney stood when Carol bounded out of her chair. "You'll do no such thing. I have my own plan."

"Aha! Strategy. So it's war, after all."

Brittney didn't like the implication. She wasn't out to defeat him. Maybe they'd join forces. They just might make an unbeatable team. All she had to do was convince him.

Laughing, Carol went upstairs to dress for her outing, leaving Brittney deep in thought. Sitting back down, Brittney heard Carol speak to Mrs. Montclair as they passed on the stairs. In a second, the older woman entered the breakfast room.

"Good morning, Brittney," she said. She went to the sideboard and poured coffee into a Lennox cup with an Oriental design, then sat at the table. "It looks nice for paddling about the lake, doesn't it?"

Mrs. Montclair was dressed in casual pink slacks, a white shell and a long-sleeved print blouse. She wore white sneakers on her petite feet.

"Is Mr. Sanders taking you canoeing?" Brittney asked.

"Yes. We're going on a nature jaunt with Carol and Harry. Are you joining us?"

A gleam came into Brittney's eyes. "I might. I'll let you know. Excuse me, please." She dashed up to her room and made two phone calls. Shortly after she heard Carol and Mrs. Montclair leave, she went downstairs and paused outside the study.

With a racing pulse, she pounded on the door. "Ready to go?" she yelled at the portal.

No answer.

"Daniel, I know you're in there."

She raised her fist to beat on the door once more. It opened, and she almost fell inside.

"I'm reading reports," he said in what she could only describe as a snarl.

"It's Sunday. You have Monday through Friday to read reports. The weekend is for family and fun." She put her hands on her hips and glared at him just as sternly as he glared at her.

It was a standoff, Daniel decided. He ought to take her up on her courtship declaration. That would teach her a lesson. Hell, she'd had a crush on him for years. A little real passion from a man and she'd run for cover. Yeah, he'd better settle this once and for all; let her get it out of her system.

Then they could become friends. Or else she'd hate him forever. That gave him pause. He liked having her around. She acted as a curb on Carol. Brittney was sensible—that is, she'd always seemed sensible until lately.

Irritated by all this tortured reasoning, he ran an impatient hand through his hair. Truthfully, he didn't know what to do. Glancing at her belligerent pose, he knew without a doubt what he'd like to do.

He hadn't slept a wink for thinking about last night and the fever she stirred in his blood with her sweet kisses. He felt the hardening of his body. Perhaps in helping her over her wild ideas, he could get over his wild impulses, too.

"All right, kitten," he said in resignation. "What do you have in mind?"

Kitten. A nickname. An endearment. A warm rush flooded Brittney's heart. No one had ever given her a pet name. "I've rented a canoe for us."

"Give me five minutes to change."

He returned the report to the desk and called Muggs on the intercom to tell him they were leaving and would be out for the day. Then he bounded up the stairs three at a time. In three minutes he was back, dressed in shorts and a polo shirt. He wore a billed cap. He handed a straw hat to her.

"Are you going in those?" he asked, indicating her slacks.

"Uh-huh. The sun is bad for—"

"Yeah, I know." He turned her with his hands on her shoulders and headed her for the door. "Are you a bossy woman?"

"I don't know. I've never had anyone to boss."

He flicked her a sidewise glance but said nothing. They walked down the lane, the shadows of leaves lacy on the pavement. Brittney put the straw hat on when they reached the marina.

"You have a reservation for Brittney Chapel," she told the young man on the dock.

"Right. Here it is. Two life jackets are under the seat. The cooler is in the back. Fill out this form." He handed her a clipboard.

She wrote in the information, gave him a check for the full amount and climbed into the canoe. "Cast off," she ordered.

Daniel did as told. When they were safely away from the pier, he asked, "Who made you captain and me mate?"

"When you make the date, you can be in charge." She saw Carol and Harry. "Hey, wait up!" she yelled. "Faster," she told Daniel.

They paddled alongside the other couple and exchanged greetings.

"We're going to picnic at the day-use area. Are you joining us?" Carol asked.

"My date forgot lunch," Daniel grumbled, peeking into the cooler, which held several cans of fruit juice and soda.

"No, I didn't."

He looked at Brittney, then did a visual search of the boat. "I know. You have two pills in your pocket that, when you add water, will swell up into a platter of fried chicken, boiled eggs, tomatoes and a bottle of wine."

"Wrong." She grinned happily at him.

"I'm to buy lunch."

"Nope."

His eyes narrowed. "We're going to forage in the woods."

She shook her head. "It's a surprise. Paddle on, my man. Time's a-wasting." She bent her back to the paddle.

"Well, we're not sharing any of our goodies with you," Carol said. "Race you to the point." She and Harry shot forward.

"Let 'em go," Daniel advised. "I'm out for a leisurely tour. This is supposed to be fun, isn't it?"

Brittney glanced over her shoulder at him. "Aren't you having fun yet, Daniel?"

He didn't answer right away. She looked back again. The intensity in his eyes caused another rush of her blood. She wondered if a person could develop high blood pressure just from being around another.

"Yes," he said softly, "the time of my life."

"Me, too." She gave him a long, level gaze, then smiled saucily at him. She hoped he liked her surprise.

They caught up with Carol and Harry, then with Beatrice and Hank. Hank had a bird book, and they took turns identifying the ducks and water birds on the lake until it was time for lunch.

At one, they put in at the picnic area. Brittney checked her watch. Perfect. Now, if her order would only arrive on time.

It did.

Five minutes after they stepped out of the canoe, a van pulled up. The driver hopped out and brought a box over to Brittney when she waved at him. She gave him the money and took the box to the table where Carol and Beatrice spread out ham and cheese, rolls and fruit on a cloth.

"Pizza," Daniel said. "Now, why didn't I think of that?"

"Takes a brilliant mind." Brittney opened the box, found paper plates and napkins, just as she'd ordered, and loaded a big slice of pizza on a plate. She placed it in front of Daniel, then fixed one for herself.

She bit into the cheesy crust and met Daniel's eyes across the table. The air was suddenly brighter, as if the sunlight had spun a golden halo around them. Their glances held . . . and held.

"That really smells good." Harry cast a hungry look at the huge pizza. "Are you two going to eat all of it?"

"You may have a piece," Brittney said graciously.

All the food was passed around, and the six of them were soon laughing and talking with the ease of long friendship. Brittney noticed Hank's eyes strayed often to Beatrice. The older woman had a very pretty flush on her cheeks. So far, so good.

After eating, they cleaned up the debris and headed around the lake once more. Late that afternoon they arrived back at the resort, returned the canoes and had drinks on the patio while they watched the sun go down.

"Hasn't this been better than reading reports?" Brittney asked Daniel when he settled back in his chair with a sigh.

"So far," he agreed.

"We may be sorry when our muscles protest getting out of bed in the morning," Hank suggested. He rotated his shoulders.

Brittney was aware of Daniel's lazy perusal of her. She wished they were alone. She wanted his kiss, his hands roaming over her as they had last night.

Her longing must have shown in her face. His expression hardened, and he turned to Hank and Harry to discuss the contract he planned to sign and return to his attorney the next day.

"So," Harry crowed, "we'll be in business together." His gaze went to Carol. "Great."

Brittney wanted to warn him not to get his hopes up about Carol. Looking at Hank, she knew the older man had cautioned the younger one. Would it do any good? *Poor Harry.*

Poor Brittney came the echo from deep inside. She frowned in perplexity. She wasn't love-dazed. In fact, she was having a very good time chasing her elusive quarry. *Poor Daniel* was more like it.

They decided to meet again for a late dinner and dancing under the stars at the resort's Esplanade Room. Brittney was glad she'd brought an extra case of evening clothes; she was accustomed to Beatrice's extravagant entertaining.

What she wasn't used to, she admitted, pinning up her hair that night, was Daniel's constant attendance. Even though she'd started their intrigue, having Daniel as a steady escort was as nerve-racking as it was exhilarating.

Feeling like one of the original Foolish Virgins, she went down and joined the rest of the group. Tonight she was the last one to arrive in the library.

Daniel brought her a glass of tonic water. "Over ice, with a twist of lemon," he murmured, his voice playing havoc with her composure.

In a white dinner jacket and black silk tie, with a rose-bud in his lapel, he looked like a hero out of a suspense book, bent on danger, and to hell with the consequences. When his gaze burned its way over her aquamarine silk dress, she felt like the heroine.

The gauzy material had a deep V neckline and was gathered in soft tucks at the waist, falling just below her knees in a swishy flounce that moved each time she did. She felt light and fluttery, like the fireflies she could see in the meadow, and her senses were on edge, as if she was expecting something to happen.

For just a moment, tears threatened to fall. Whatever was wrong with her? Impatient with her shaky emotions, she turned her back to the room after speaking to the others and walked to the window. More fireflies joined the first.

Daniel approached. She felt the warmth of his body as he stopped right behind her, not touching, but no more than an inch away. "What are you looking at?" he asked, his voice deep and quiet, soothing her unrest.

She nodded toward the meadow. "The fireflies. They look like fairies, leaping and dancing to some primitive music we mortals can't hear."

"Can't we?"

His breath caressed her hair. "Can you?" she asked.

"Only when you're around."

With a parting glance, he moved away, once more the congenial host seeing to his guests' needs. Although she knew he was playing her game, she wished his statement was true.

They walked down to the resort shortly thereafter. She and Daniel strolled behind the other couples as they had previously. Brittney noticed the scent of his after-shave, crisp and fresh but with subtle undertones of woods and meadows that suited him.

Her senses were especially acute tonight. She had never seen so many stars, so many fireflies, had never known such magic in the air. She breathed deeply of the invisible elixir and felt the breeze glide across her bare shoulders like a lover's caress.

They had wine on the patio under a sliver of moon while wandering musicians played haunting Gypsy music on violins. At eight, they were called to their table on the glassed-in terrace overlooking the lake.

Beatrice asked Hank what he thought was the best fish item on the menu. He went over each dish with her until a decision was reached, then gave the order to the waiter. Carol and Harry, after stating their preferences, drifted off to speak to one of her many friends in the restaurant.

"I hope he moves here permanently," Daniel told Brittney, indicating Hank, who was deep in a discussion of favorite foods with Beatrice.

"He is good for your sister-in-law," she observed. "He likes being consulted and taking charge. I should think most men would."

"Not me. I have enough decisions to make on the job. I don't want to be bothered with someone else's, too."

She filed that bit of information away. He would expect his wife to handle her responsibilities without drawing him into it. She had been trained to do just that by one of the most exacting women of Southern tradition. That tradition demanded a man be made comfortable in his home without bothering his head over domestic details. Behind the scenes, "the little woman" ruled the household with a steel scepter. Brittney could handle it. She'd observed her mother often enough.

"Do you need guidance?" he suddenly asked.

She laughed. "Well, my mother thinks I do, but I've never taken very well to being told what to do."

He seemed to find this disclosure amusing. "Until recently, I saw you as an obedient child, perhaps docile."

"And now?" "Docile" didn't sound very flattering.

"Now I think I underestimated you. That quiet, pleasant exterior is a cover for..." He ran the tip of his finger along her cheek while he looked deep into her eyes.

"For?" she prodded, impatient to hear his thoughts.

"Other traits."

She was disappointed by his evasion. "What other traits?"

"Persistence, possibly stubbornness," he answered. "With a tendency to get wild ideas. And act upon them. There's also passion and fire." His voice dropped to a husky rumble on the last statement.

He was attracted. She could see it in his eyes—the male interest, the hunger. Warning bells ricocheted along her spine. She ignored them.

Returning his perusal, she reached for his hand and brought it to her lips. With the lightest touch, she kissed his fingers, each one of them, then nibbled at the tips, her eyes never leaving his face.

His exhaled breath was an admission of defeat. He withdrew his hand from hers. "You're burning holes right through all my good intentions," he warned.

She gave him an impudent grin. "I'm not the least interested in your good intentions. Now, maybe your bad ones..."

Later, when the orchestra played, they danced. She hummed the popular love song and flirted with Daniel with her eyes. She made it clear she saw no other man in the room.

"Playing the vamp, kitten?" he asked one time.

"Just making sure you know I'm present," she replied, whirling away from him and coming back into his arms. "'Come to me in the moonlight,'" she sang softly to him. "'Fill me with flaming desire. Come to me in the moonlight. Darling, my heart's on fire.'"

"I hope you know what you're doing," he muttered. "I sure as hell don't."

"Yes, you do. I told you—I'm courting you."

"Like hell," he said.

"Umm, that is one way you could look at it."

The clock in the library struck midnight when Brittney slipped out of her room. She was dressed for seduction. At least, she thought she was. Her dark blue satin nightgown and robe skimmed over her curves like silken veils.

Going outside, she picked up a few pebbles from a flower box and lobbed them at Daniel's window. It took five tries before he opened the French doors and stepped out on the balcony.

"What are you doing?" he demanded.

He was wonderfully handsome in pajama bottoms and tousled hair and not at all like his daytime self. She liked the "night" Daniel better than the "day" one. He didn't look so tough.

"Serenading you."

She turned on the tape in her boom box. "'Come to me in the moonlight,'" she pantomimed the song. "'Fill me with flaming desire. Come to me in the moonlight. Darling, my heart's on fire.'"

Daniel leaned his arms on the railing and watched her lip-synch the recording. Then he climbed over the balcony and dropped lightly to the ground.

"Now," he said.

Taking the tape player from her, he placed it on the edge of the flowerpot. The music started again. With a sweeping turn, he pulled Brittney into his arms and waltzed her around the lawn, their bare feet making no sound on the warm grass.

She dropped her head back and laughed up at the moon. His lips caught her in the act, going straight for her throat. He kissed a blazing path along all the sensitive points as he traced the slender line of bone to her shoulder and back.

"Daniel," she whispered.

"What do you want, Brittney? Tell me. I'm yours to command," he said huskily between teasing nips along the cords of her neck. He reached her ear and took the lobe in his mouth.

"I want you to love me. Make love to me, Daniel."

"And then?"

"We'll face that tomorrow," she said.

"You tempt a man beyond reason."

He held her away from him. She smiled tentatively.

"Is it that bad, kitten?" he demanded hoarsely. "Is this the first time you've been caught by desire? It's an instinct as old as time, as demanding as self-preservation, and damned hard to deny, isn't it?" He gave her a firm shake, wanting an answer.

"Yes."

He muttered an expletive, then crushed her to him. "All right," he said against her hair. "All right."

He ignored the argument going on inside him, telling him he was getting in over his head. If they made love, he'd feel compelled to marry her. A warning rang in his ears.

No way. She knew the score. She'd started this game. It was time she learned she was in the big leagues now. They'd play by his rules.

She's courting you, dummy. That's marriage in any book.

His lips came down on hers, hard and unyielding, wringing every last drop of desire from her trembling body. His hands roamed restlessly over her back until he cupped her hips and brought her into intimate contact with his hunger.

She clutched his shoulders, then slid her hands around him, caressing and pressing him closer. Need sizzled inside him like a sparkler. God, he loved her touch.

Brittney heard the small sound he made, a groan of torture. She knew the feeling. With every breath she wanted him closer.

His pajamas had elastic in the waistband. She could easily slip her hands inside. She did and felt the hard, smooth muscles of his hips flex under her questing fingers. He was strong, so strong; all masculine lines and planes. A sculpture of the finest marble come to life in her arms in the moonlight.

Caught up in her whimsy, she forgot everything but the moment. He started moving even while he kissed her, and they danced slowly to the music, around and around, until she was dizzy.

"Ah, Brittney," he said, his kisses wild on her face. He carried her to a chair in the deep shadows on the patio and held her on his lap. Her hair fell across his arm as she lay back and looked up at him.

He touched her face with one finger, the way he had in the restaurant. Tracing a sensuous circuit, he drew curlicues on her skin from her cheek, down her neck, to her chest. Slowly he blazed a path to her breast. With a lazy movement, he circled her hardened nipple.

"Is this what you want, kitten? Touching and kissing?"

"Yes." She closed her eyes, unable to stand the ecstasy.

He pushed her robe aside and cupped her breasts, first one, then the other. She gasped as heat flowed into her. With slow movements, he pulled down the blue satin gown until one breast gleamed like dull silver in the dark night.

She reached up and stroked his chest, searching through the hair until she could feel his response in the hard dots of his own nipples. "Are you sensitive there, too?" she asked.

"I have feelings there," he admitted.

Smiling, she leaned forward to kiss the tiny points and felt his stomach muscles contract against her. Fascinated, she continued her experiment in male sexuality by kissing his throat the way he'd done hers earlier.

"This is new to you, isn't it?"

"Umm," she said, running her hands over him. She was aware of his desire beneath her thighs.

"You want to touch and taste, perhaps test my reactions and compare them to the boys you've known. *This* is a man's passion."

His tone warned her a second before he pushed her gently against his arm and dropped his mouth to her breast. He sucked greedily, causing wave upon wave of sensation to cascade through her. It was wonderful, different from anything she'd ever known.

Because of her former infatuation for Daniel, she had held herself aloof from her dates, although more than one had tried to break through her reserve. But with Daniel there was no need for caution. From him she wanted everything...everything!

He caressed her other breast, his tongue and lips alternately pulling and sliding against her sensitive flesh. When she couldn't stand it another second, he lifted his head. He stared into her dazed eyes, then smiled.

"You liked that."

She nodded.

He covered a breast with one hand. He slipped the other under her hair until he could cup her head and bring her mouth to his. "Give me your mouth, kitten. I want to taste you."

His tongue stroked her lips for invitation. She had no thought of withholding anything from him. She opened her mouth and let him inside. They played, warred, danced... She wasn't sure of the term, only that she loved the intimate mingling. It made her want more.

When he released her lips, they both breathed heavily, sucking in air while they waited for their pulses to still somewhat.

"We need to go in," he said.

"Take me to your room."

Daniel started up with her held tightly in his arms. He would have fought a pride of lions to claim her, but there was nothing that physical at hand. Instead, his conscience pricked him.

She's innocent, and she's thinking of marriage.

He sighed and knew he couldn't take from her that which belonged to another man—the husband she wanted. He wasn't that person, and he couldn't pretend to be in order to satisfy his own lust. Slowly he let her slide from his arms, her body leaving trails of fire along his.

"Save your passion, kitten, for the man who deserves it. Now get in the house."

He released her before she knew what was happening. The radio was turned off and pressed into her hands, and she was escorted into the house.

He opened her door and shoved her gently inside. His smile flashed in the gloom. "Keep looking at me like that and I might think it's worth sending my soul to hell to stay with you."

With that, he closed the door and was gone.

She yanked it open and called softly to his back, "Maybe it would be." She closed the door then, and, on second thought, locked it.

Chapter Five

Daniel wasn't at the table Monday morning when Brittney came down. She hadn't expected him to be. She'd slept late, and by now he would be at the printing-company office. After eating a bowl of cereal, she sipped her tea and looked over the listings of apartments. She was busy circling those that sounded good when Carol appeared, dressed attractively in tennis togs.

"Hi, see anything?" she asked.

"Good morning. Several sound okay," Brittney said. "Do you have time to go look this afternoon?"

"I have a better idea. Daniel knows a fellow in real estate whose office handles rental units. Let's ask for their listings. We'd get addresses and details that way."

"Oh, that is a good idea."

Carol grinned modestly. "Well, I do come up with one once in a while. I'll call Daniel. He can get the list and bring it home tonight. We can go over it after dinner."

"No date with Harry?"

"Yes. He can help us."

Brittney laughed. "Just what he wants—to spend an evening with us, pouring over apartments."

Her friend shrugged. "If he gets bored, he can leave."

"He won't." Brittney knew Carol could make an evening of reading the telephone book seem exciting. "Will you call Daniel?"

Carol gave her an assessing glance. "All not well in Eden? Don't answer that. It's none of my business. Yes, I'll call. Right after breakfast."

She ate half a grapefruit, then toast and scrambled eggs and finally a bran muffin before settling back with a sigh. "Pour me some coffee," she requested. "I'll make the call."

Brittney fixed the coffee for Carol and replenished her own cup of tea. She waited impatiently for Carol to reappear. Who she really wanted to appear was Daniel, but she'd see him tonight when he returned from work.

What if he decided to stay over at his penthouse?

She grimaced. That was one place she wouldn't go without an invitation from Daniel—his bachelor lair. Though she'd certainly like to change that!

Letting herself drift into daydreams, she pictured them here at the big house, their children scampering on the grass. Daniel's eyes would meet hers, and they'd both remember the night they'd danced in the moonlight...and fallen madly in love.

She sighed dreamily. Sometime during the night her goal had changed. Her courtship was real, not an effort at revenge. She wanted marriage with Daniel.

Love is a smoke, raised in a fume of sighs. Being purged, a fire sparkling in lover's eyes.... The poet had known the tender, tormenting emotion well. And so did she. If she had her way, Daniel would know it, too.

Carol returned. From the frown on her friend's face, Brittney braced herself for bad news.

"Daniel has fled," she said dramatically.

"Fled?" Brittney's mind couldn't grasp the term.

"For the north country. His secretary said he dropped off the printing contracts and took off to see about the logging operation. Some nature radicals are spiking the trees."

Brittney's immediate reaction was fear for Daniel's safety. She knew the danger of spiked logs. When a saw blade hit the embedded spikes, the blade would shear. The fast-spinning pieces of steel and wood could blind, maim or kill a person.

"When will Daniel return?" Brittney asked, her face composed, her voice deceptively quiet.

"Who knows? Daniel's secretary knew which real estate agent I meant. She'll get the info and mail it to us. There, problem all solved. Now we can play tennis this afternoon. The club is getting up a round-robin," Carol finished.

Brittney forced herself to smile. "Who's playing?"

"Mom and Hank, Harry and I. We'll find a partner—"

"Would you be offended if I begged off? I'd like to laze around and finish a book I started ages ago."

Carol started to protest, but she was a live-and-let-live person who didn't require her guests to attend every activity she planned. Brittney was grateful when Carol smiled and agreed to let her off the hook this time.

They chatted amiably about the romance between Beatrice and Hank. When her mother appeared, Carol teased her about her "boyfriend." Beatrice blushed so profusely that her daughter was startled into silence.

"It must be serious," Carol whispered when her mother left to get ready for the tennis tournament.

"I think it is," Brittney agreed. Sympathetic to the love affairs of others, she fervently hoped everything worked out for them. "Would you be upset if they married?"

Carol looked startled yet again. She thought it over and shook her head. "Hank seems nice. I think I'd be glad for them. If he's good to her." She paused, frowned, then smiled. "He wouldn't dare not be. Daniel would kill him if Mother was hurt." So saying, she sprang out of her chair and dashed off to put on her tennis shoes, calling a farewell over her shoulder.

Brittney drifted out to the patio. Sitting on the broad concrete railing, she let the sun warm her while she admitted the downward turn of her spirits at Daniel's departure. He could have told her instead of letting her find out this way. Unless, of course, he was running from her.

She knew he'd enjoyed himself with her over the weekend. At least he had some of the time, she acknowledged truthfully. He'd also been angry at her. But that had been because he had tried to deny his desire for her. When he had yielded to it... She closed her eyes in remembered rapture.

When he had yielded to it, they had shared an ecstasy that had been wonderful.

Save your passion, kittens, for the man who deserves it.

Ah, Daniel, don't you know you are that man—only you and no other? She wished she could make him see that.

Did he care?

She thought he did. He wasn't a cruel person, although he did tend to be a loner. He was indulgent and patient with Beatrice and Carol, but at times during the years she'd known them, she'd sensed his exasperation with them when they acted foolishly.

Both women, she suddenly realized, had been pampered in ways she hadn't. Was she envious? Her own mother and grandfather had been strict with her, each in a different way.

Her mother had expected restraint, proper decorum and certain capabilities required of a gentlewoman. Her grandfather had demanded fiscal responsibility, clear thinking and good judgment. Each loved her in his or her own way, she thought, although she had at times felt like the rope in a tug-of-war between them.

But the love of a parent wasn't the love of a husband. She wanted her life to be a tapestry, a rich weaving of passion with love, friendship, children and all that marriage promised.

What did Daniel's abrupt departure mean? The problem in the north could be serious enough to need his immediate attention. Or he could be running from his own emotions. Her spirits perked up. Perhaps she had cracked the wall of his reserve. Perhaps he was falling in love with her....

"So, what were you reading today that was more important than the tennis match?" Harry demanded.

Brittney smiled at him. "A book of poetry. Seventeenth-century British."

"Those people were bawdy," Carol interjected, sweeping into the room. She was dressed in a rose trouser suit with a white silk blouse. She and Harry were going to a nightclub. "We're talking serious smut," she confided in low tones. "You should read some of those poems and find out what they were up to."

Brittney laughed at the startled expression on Harry's face. "No more so than *The Canterbury Tales*," she defended.

"Well, there you have it." Carol whirled on Harry. "That Wife of Bath was a floozy. Don't you agree?"

"Well, uh..." He was obviously racking his brain to remember who the Wife of Bath was and what she'd done.

Brittney took pity on him and answered in his place. "She was truthful. She called 'em as she saw 'em."

"And boy, did she see 'em."

She and Carol exchanged an amused look. During their school years, they had argued over a multitude of ideas and morals presented in books and essays.

After the couple left, Brittney sat in an easy chair and rocked back and forth. What was a virgin but a person who hadn't yet sampled all of life? That was probably what had sent Daniel away. He had found her inexperience amusing to a point, but . . .

He was the cause of it, she protested—as if he were present to hear her reasoning. The young men in college had been insipid next to Daniel's charm and intriguing intensity. They had seemed as flighty and raucous as jaybirds.

A car entered the drive. Hank got out and came to the door. Muggs answered the bell and called for Beatrice. In a minute Brittney heard the car leave.

She didn't know how long she sat there. The sunset faded and the long twilight of the northern climes lingered, leaving the room in deepening shadows. Her mind drifted in a haze, not really thinking. She wouldn't admit to feeling sad or lonely. Instead she seemed to be in an emotional limbo where nothing mattered and nothing could touch her. Perhaps life was easier that way. The ringing of the phone shattered her quiet.

Muggs came into the room and turned on a lamp. He told her Daniel was on the line.

"Does he want to talk to me?" she asked, surprised.

Muggs nodded and left.

She lifted the receiver. "Hello, Daniel." In the pause before he spoke, she could hear the hard beating of her heart and wondered if she'd always react to him this way.

"Hello, Brittney. Muggs said you were there alone. Where are the others off to?"

There was an odd tone in his voice. She tried to figure it out, but couldn't. "Well, Carol and Harry are going to catch a cabaret act at a nightclub, and Beatrice and Harry are joining another couple for bridge. The Rostaners, I think she said."

Silence followed her cheery listing of events. "What about you?" he finally demanded.

"What about me?"

"Didn't anyone think to ask you along?"

She caught the undertone. He was angry at Beatrice and Carol for leaving her, their guest, on her own. Daniel, the considerate host, who took all his responsibilities so seriously. She didn't want to be seen as another of his problems. "As a matter of fact, they all did. I preferred to read—"

"In the dark?"

"I beg your pardon?"

"Muggs said you were sitting in the dark."

"Oh. Well, it was peaceful. Until you called," she teased, lightening the tone of their conversation. "You don't have to worry about me, Daniel. I'm an adult. I can take care of my own amusements." She changed the subject. "How's it going? Did you find any spiked logs?"

"Not yet. Everything is under control. We thought some demonstrators were going to show up and throw themselves under the equipment, but no one did." He gave an exasperated snort. "My men said they were going to run over anything on the road, so I thought I'd better come up to keep things cool."

"I'm sure you're good at that."

"Was that a cynical remark?" he asked, his voice going soft and doing things to her senses.

"Take it any way you like."

"I think I'd like to take it with a— No, I'd better not say with what." He laughed. "You've interrupted my sleep."

"If I were with you, you might sleep better," she suggested. She was surprised at just how provocative she could be.

"Would you sing me a lullaby?" He spoke in the same tone she had used: sexy, semiserious and challenging.

"Yes, among other things." She didn't elaborate.

He sighed, then laughed. "I can see I'm going to have another difficult night. Tell Beatrice to call me tomorrow about the Fourth of July party."

"Are you going to be gone until then?" She was disappointed. It would be over a week before she saw him again.

"Yes." He was back to being curt.

"Well, take care. And don't take up with any floozies," she ordered sternly.

"We don't have many up here in the woods," he said dryly. "Good night, Brittney."

"Good night." She hung up.

He was back to being a relative of a friend. Would he ever call her "kitten" again?

Darn right, he would!

"A bunch of fake cowboys," Carol remarked, looking over the crowd on the lawn.

"And cowgirls," Brittney added in a sense of fairness.

"True."

Carol looked at her own clothes and laughed. She and Brittney were dressed in jeans, sneakers and Western shirts with mother-of-pearl snaps instead of buttons. Bandannas were rolled and tied around their foreheads, giving a modern flair to their outfits.

The Fourth of July party was in full swing. It was nearly six o'clock. Dinner would be served soon. A huge side of pork turned on a spit, its juices sizzling on the charcoal below. Nearby, tables were covered with food, which was already being sampled.

A crowd of people, about two hundred, moseyed around the yard, eating and drinking, laughing and talking. Horseshoes, badminton and volleyball games were in progress. A hayride was planned for later, when the moon rose.

Brittney looked forward to the night. The moonlight seemed to relax Daniel's vigilance on his emotions and drive him into her arms. He had returned to the lake house only last night, coming in late, after everyone was in bed. She had tried to stay up for him, but sleep had overcome her.

Today she'd only caught glimpses of him as he circulated among his guests, many of them workers from Montclair Enterprises. Only once had she found his eyes on her.

"Well, let's mingle, shall we?" Carol stepped off the patio onto the grass.

"Did you invite Harry?"

"Yes. He and Hank will be here later. I thought we'd eat together. Join us?"

"Maybe."

Carol laughed. "Waiting for Daniel to ask?"

"Nope." Brittney just smiled. "See you later."

She wandered off, her course seemingly aimless. She walked to a spot in Daniel's line of vision, but not too close. With the grace of long practice, she chatted with a couple who looked ill at ease in the casual but elegant setting.

"What department are you in?" she inquired, having learned the man worked at the printing company.

"Accounting," he replied.

"He was recently promoted to manager of accounts payable," his wife added. She immediately looked as if she wished she hadn't spoken.

"Congratulations," Brittney said warmly. Turning to the wife, she remarked, "That's a lovely outfit. Wherever did you find it?"

The woman wore a ruffled skirt with stiff net petticoats under it. The pink gingham checks went well with her blond coloring. She looked wholesome. "I made it."

Brittney examined a section of lace. "Really! You must be a wonderful seamstress. My mother made me learn, but my seams always looked like they'd been done by a blind person in the dark."

They laughed and talked comfortably for several minutes. Then Brittney called over a couple of people she knew from previous visits and included them in the conversation. When things were going well, she slipped away.

Turning, she looked directly at Daniel. He was watching her, his expression guarded. She smiled, batted her lashes and walked away. One of the caterers was trying to decide where to place the dessert table. She suggested a location. Going into the library, she returned with a vase of roses and placed them on the table.

She swung around and looked at Daniel with a question in her eyes after pointing at the flowers. *Is this okay?*

He nodded.

She smiled again and looked for her next project. An elderly lady was trapped in conversation with another woman who wouldn't let her get a word in. She looked desperate to get away.

"Excuse me—" Brittney interrupted the talkative one "—did I hear you say you'd been to England last year?"

"Yes, I went with my church group—"

"Wonderful. I know someone who is dying to go but would like some information." She took the woman's arm and led her away. "He'd love to talk to you." She left the woman happily telling old Mr. Parker—who couldn't hear a word but would sit patiently for hours while others talked—about her adventure.

A warm hand clasped her upper arm. "What do you think you're doing?" Daniel asked.

"Being a hostess. Do you know that Southern women are the best in the world?"

"Is that so?"

He tucked his thumbs under his belt and studied her for a moment or two. Brittney thought he looked wonderful in his jeans and blue chambray shirt. They looked like real work clothes rather than the fashionable attire of his guests. The material was soft and faded and looked as if it had gotten that way naturally.

"Is that your logging outfit?" she asked.

"I sometimes wear this at the camp." He pushed a dark wave off his forehead. He took her arm again and guided her toward the barbecue pit. "Why are you trying to impress me with your hostess skills?"

"I thought you might need to know. A big-shot executive would have to entertain a lot, wouldn't he?" She gave him an oblique glance to see if he'd caught the implication.

"Still shooting for the M.R.S.?"

"Yes." She refused to be daunted by the thunderheads of anger gathering in his eyes.

"I'm not the marrying kind." His tone was kind. It made her furious.

"Why not? People do it all the time."

"From what I've seen, they end up hating each other. It's a shackle I don't intend to don."

"It doesn't have to be that way. If two people respect each other's space—"

"Are you in love with me, Brittney?"

She went very still at the question. She hadn't expected it and had no answer prepared.

"Why, Daniel, a gentleman doesn't pry into a woman's heart." It took an effort, but she laughed lightly. "Unless he's offering his own in return. Are you?"

He snorted. "I have enough problems without taking on more." With a smile that devastated her heart, he tugged on the end of the bandanna. "You want starry-eyed romance. And you think you want me. But I'm not for you. Find a younger man who still has his ideals intact."

"What happened to yours?" she demanded boldly.

"They faced up to reality."

He stroked his hands along her upper arms in a sweet caress. She was sure he didn't realize he was doing it. "Do you look at marriage as a trap?"

"It's a responsibility I don't want. I come and go a lot. I don't get home for dinner at the same time every night. I catch up on my reading in the evening instead of going out. I don't bare my soul or share my every thought."

She tilted her head to one side. "A wife would be good for you, I think. You work too hard. You need someone to teach you to relax and enjoy the other things in life." With a come-hither glance, she added in a husky tone, "Like dancing in the moonlight. You enjoyed that, Daniel."

"I enjoyed what I thought it was leading to," he told her in blunt terms.

"You were the one who pulled back."

"I told you my reasons." His voice dropped an octave. He leaned closer to her. His hands slid across her shoulders and circled her neck. He caressed her throat with callused thumbs. "Do you think I'd take your gift without giving anything back? What kind of man would do that?"

"What kind?" she immediately asked.

Daniel saw the challenge in her eyes. Her lashes, which were long and thick and beautiful, cast shadows on her cheeks when she looked down. When she looked back at him, they swept up in a way that turned him on. It was all he could do not to kiss her.

"One that I'd shoot," he vowed, feeling tender toward her.

"You don't have to watch out for me, Daniel. I'm a big girl." She put her hands on his wrists. "Is it because I haven't—"

"No," he broke in. "Your virginity isn't the factor. Don't you remember? I told you to save your passion for the man who deserved it. That's your gift. The sweet, urgent, unbelievable passion you showed me that night."

Brittney felt the heat burn into her face. Unless he wrote it in one of his infernal reports, he couldn't have made it clearer that he didn't want her gift.

"Give it to someone who will offer the things you need from life. Women need marriage and security. I realize that."

She pulled away from him. Anger simmered just beneath the surface of her control. "Men have needs, too. Marriage can be just as beneficial for the male of the species as the female."

"Name one benefit," he snapped, losing his patience with her.

"We could make love any time we wanted."

"Damn. You don't mind hitting below the belt, do you?"

"If that's what it takes." She smiled at him. "All's fair, Daniel." Her voice was husky, promising, tempting.

"I could have taken you that night we danced. You wouldn't have said no." He regarded her with frosty eyes.

She didn't reply to his statement, which was probably true, but spoke her own thoughts. "It isn't the idea of having a wife that you dislike. It's the idea of being shackled. You don't want to answer to anyone for your actions. I understand," she assured him.

"That's right. I don't." He crossed his arms over his chest, looking wholly, fiercely, independently masculine.

She reached up and caressed his lean cheek. "Don't blame me if you end up a lonely old bachelor." With a smile, she walked off, leaving him standing there with his arguments on the tip of his tongue and no one to tell them to.

Chapter Six

Brittney sat with Carol and Harry during dinner. Daniel sat with the managers from the Montclair companies. She met Ed Zimm, who was the real estate agent helping with her apartment hunting. So far, she hadn't seen anything she liked from the list in the paper.

"I have several you should check," Ed told her. "We can look at them Monday. Shall I come by for you at ten?"

"Would you mind? I don't have a car yet. That's next on my list." She grimaced, thinking of all the items necessary to set up a household, and hoped her money would hold out.

"No problem."

Later in the evening, the band showed up and set up their equipment. The amplifiers were so loud, she feared for her hearing. Daniel, with his usual competency, had them turn the volume to a reasonable level.

"Dance?" Ed asked.

They went together to the temporary dance pavilion that had been placed on the lawn near the lake. The number was fast, and she discovered Ed was a gifted dancer.

He was handsome in a well-kept manner. His hair was stylish, his clothes smooth-fitting and his nails buffed. There were no calluses on his hands. She suspected he was vain about his looks.

When the tune was over, she and Carol swapped partners. Harry was equally good on the dance floor—very smooth and polished. As the music segued into a slow melody, a hand tapped imperiously on Harry's shoulder.

"My turn, I think."

Daniel took the younger man's place. Instead of holding her in the usual manner, he ignored her outstretched hand and folded her against his hard body with both arms around her. There was no doubt in her mind that he saw her as a woman. She made a little murmuring sound as she nestled contentedly against him.

Being in Daniel's arms filled her with the same sense of pleasure she felt each time she visited the lake house—a sense of homecoming. She'd always felt that she belonged here.

A stillness grew inside her. She realized just how much she loved this man. She'd never stopped loving Daniel.

Only now, she didn't feel just the tingle of girlish wonder when he looked at her. She experienced a woman's anticipation and impatience to know life at its fullest. She wanted all of him.

And she wanted to give him all that she was—all her love and passion, with no holding back.

She wanted all that the future would allow with this hard, rugged man from the north country.

With an effort, she smiled lightly at him. "Our third dance," she whispered for his ears alone.

Daniel felt the full effect of her eyes on him. She was sexy and beautiful by any standard. She looked dreamy and happy. A lump formed in his throat. Did he do this to her?

Other women had wanted him. They had also wanted the power of his position or the luxury of his money or the influence of his contacts. Brittney wanted only him.

The sense of tenderness that she stirred in him returned. He wanted to wrap himself around this sweet bundle of femininity and hide her in a safe place.

Bah! This was probably all part of her ploy to drive him insane . . . or into marriage. Marriage, the tender trap, with *trap* being the operative word.

"You can knock off the soulful glances," he said. "I'm not falling for it, and I'm not getting married."

He saw the happiness disappear. A flicker of hurt passed over her face, then she said quite gently, "You must, of course, do as you think best, Daniel."

She became aloof and stayed that way until the end of the dance. When it was over, she whirled away from him, her hips moving seductively in her formfitting jeans. He felt a moment's regret for his harshness. She was still young. Why not let her keep her dreams awhile longer?

Brittney shook her head. "No, this won't do."

"Fair enough," Ed said. "We have time for one more, then we'll go to lunch."

"Fine."

They inspected another apartment, then went downtown.

She reviewed her situation while he maneuvered through the traffic. Her salary wasn't going to be enough for even the most modest of places, she realized, disheartened by this fact.

Ed pulled into a parking space at one of Minneapolis's more expensive restaurants. He took her arm as they went inside and leaned solicitously over her. He was a charming, practiced male, and she appreciated his attention. Her ego needed it.

Last night, after one dance, Daniel had ignored her the rest of the evening. Between courting him and setting up her home, she was becoming discouraged, she admitted. Nothing was ever as easy as it seemed at first thought. Or second, or third.

She and Ed were taken to a table in the dimly lit restaurant. It took a few minutes to adjust to the near darkness. When she did, she spotted Daniel seated straight across from them, his eyes hard as pebbles as he looked at her. He was with a man and a woman.

For some reason, she couldn't summon a smile. Instead, she nodded, then turned all her attention on Ed.

"Now, let's see," he said, pulling out his list. "This one might do—"

"How much does it rent for?"

He told her.

Brittney heaved a deep sigh of disappointment. "Don't you have anything cheaper?"

"Not that you'd want to live in. The neighborhood would be dangerous." He leveled a devastating smile on her. "I'd worry about you."

She realized he was sending her signals. He'd probably been throwing out lures all morning, and she'd missed them. His ego was most likely in shreds.

"Would you excuse me?" she asked.

"Of course." He slipped out of the booth and stood until she walked away.

In the ladies' room, she touched up her lipstick and combed her hair, refastening it in a clip at the back of her neck. She stood there a few minutes, staring into space, her mind curiously empty. This courting was harder than it looked.

"Stop it," she muttered, exasperated with herself. All she thought about was Daniel. It had to stop. With this little lecture behind her, she opened the door.

When she walked out, a shadow loomed over her from behind the telephone kiosk. "Oh," she cried softly, startled.

Daniel took her arm, halting her. "What are you doing with Ed Zimm?" he demanded.

"Apartment hunting. Why?" She was perplexed by his attitude. What was he so angry about?

He didn't answer for a minute. His eyes raked up and down her slender figure. The pleats of her skirt fell in soft lines over her hips. She saw him follow the curves, then pause somewhere down her abdomen before returning to her gaze. Heat drummed into her blood. She was sure it was caused by anger.

"He's a womanizer from way back."

Her fingers tightened on her purse as if they had an itch to hit him with it. "So?"

"Dammit, he's too experienced for you."

She absorbed this information. "What's the matter, Daniel? You don't want me, but you don't want another man to have me? You can't have it both ways."

"He's already been through three wives. Are you trying to make number four?"

She tugged her arm free. "No. He's not my type. And you're not my keeper." She returned to the table.

"Everything okay?" Ed asked, peering at her flushed face.

At least the man was perceptive. Not like some hardheaded males she could name. "Fine." She gave him her best smile and flattered him with her undivided attention as they went over the rental lists yet again. She turned down dinner with him, and he took her back to the lake house.

At ten, Brittney yawned and considered going to bed. The other two women were still out on dates with Hank and Harry. Daniel hadn't come home. He was probably at the penthouse. Or out with some woman. Or with a woman at the penthouse.

Suddenly she felt very alone. Very *lonely*.

Lord, but she must have been crazy to start her campaign of revenge on Daniel. Her feminine pride had demanded that he notice her as a woman. Then she'd decided that wasn't enough. She had to have her cake and marriage, too.

He'd played fair. Right from the first. He'd told her he wasn't the marrying kind. Whatever possessed her to think she could change his mind?

She tossed her book of poetry aside and stretched out on the library sofa. Soon her lashes drifted down.

Before she could fall asleep, a car drove up. In a minute she heard footsteps in the hall. She recognized them right away. Daniel was home.

He came into the room, and she was aware of his masculine presence right away. He walked over to the sofa and peered over the back. They stared at each other. His hair was rumpled. His eyes looked tired. She wanted to soothe him, to draw his head to her breasts and kiss his cares away.

"Heavy date?" she asked instead, sitting up with her back against the padded arm and her knees drawn up to her chest.

"Work." He rubbed his eyes. "I've been going over a plan to update our printing operations. The cost is enormous."

"I see." She inhaled deeply, taking in the scents of his cologne and the warmer one that was his. The force of his maleness overwhelmed all her senses.

He looked at her for a long minute, and she saw the desire flame in his eyes until they were dark and fathomless. His longing excited all her senses to instant hunger.

He poured a glass of brandy and offered it to her. She accepted it. He poured himself another and took a drink. She sipped the rich liquid and thought of his kiss. It, too, would be rich in flavor and go straight to her head.

He sat in the easy chair and looked at her through half-closed eyes. "What are you doing here alone?"

"Waiting for you," she said softly, giving him only a hint of a smile. She felt so vulnerable.

"I figured you'd be out with the local heartthrob."

"If you mean Ed, he did ask me out to dinner."

"Why didn't you go?"

"I thought about what you said. I don't want to be anyone's number four."

He finished the brandy, stood and stretched. Then he came to her. "You want to be first, Brittney? I've had other women."

He made her wary when he loomed dark and menacing over her. Her hand fluttered to the neck of her Western shirt. She rubbed a finger over the smooth surface of the mother-of-pearl snap.

"But you haven't had me," she said.

He sat beside her all at once, scrunching her knees against her chest as he moved closer until there was no space between them. He leaned against her legs, effectively pressing her into the corner of the couch. She was trapped.

"No, I haven't. Shall I rectify that?"

"I'm not afraid of you, Daniel." Really, she wasn't, but his mood was strange, and he made her nervous. She couldn't tell what he was thinking.

"Have I ever indicated I wanted to hurt you?" he asked, lowering his face toward hers. His eyes were on her mouth.

"No, but I think you're trying to intimidate me."

"Shut up and kiss me."

"I don't think I want to kiss you. It only leaves me wanting more when you push me away."

She felt his breath touch her face as he encircled her shoulders with his arms and leaned his head over her knees. His mouth brushed hers in the most gentle way possible.

"Maybe it'll be different this time," he murmured. "Maybe I'll want you too much to stop."

Brittney sucked in a deep breath, but her denial was already slipping into oblivion. He was big, strong and warm; he seemed to encompass all of her in the intimate space between his body and the sofa. He made her feel feminine and desirable.

"Don't," she said, gasping when his tongue brushed her lips.

"Yes." His hand tangled in her hair. "Bloom for me. No, leave your mouth open."

The merging began. He fitted his lips over hers until they met in a perfect embrace. His tongue flirted with hers, darting, retreating, flicking hers again and again until she answered his challenge. When she entered his mouth, he sucked greedily.

She felt dizzy with the sensations he aroused with just a kiss. If they made love... The thought boggled the mind.

When the kiss ended, he laid his chin on her knees, his breath coming in great, ragged inhalations. He closed his eyes.

His face, so close to hers, fascinated her. It had an angular purity, a clarity of line that she found appealing. His lips, far from being inflexible, had taken many shapes against hers. They looked soft and vulnerable now, after their passionate kiss. She knew hers must be the same.

His lashes were short but thick, lying flat against the tanned skin. She leaned forward and kissed each of his eyes. When she drew back, he followed and nuzzled her nose with his.

"You make me forget there's a tomorrow," he told her huskily.

"Perhaps there isn't. Perhaps it's now or never, Daniel."

Was she teasing or not? She wasn't sure. His eyes darkened. So dark with passion, so light with laughter, she thought. She'd seen him in many different moods now, and found them all intriguing.

He fingered the pearl snaps. With a tug, one came open. He undid another. "I want to see your breasts." He glanced up and smiled. "You're blushing. Poor little virgin, so many experiences yet to be learned."

"I'm a good pupil," she parried, determined not to let him best her. She fastened her shirt. "But not tonight."

The power of his hunger washed over her, nearly destroying her defenses. She held firm. He suddenly relaxed, and his mood softened. "You're a beautiful woman. I can't deny that I want you. It's an instinct that's hard to override."

Before she could determine the best response, Beatrice and Hank returned to the house. Daniel and Brittney scrambled apart and straightened their clothing. Just like a couple of teenagers, she thought, seeing the humor in the situation. Daniel seemed to see it, too.

"Saved by fate," he whispered just as Hank and Beatrice swept into the room.

The other couple had important news. "Hank has asked me to marry him," Beatrice said, her manner at once shy and defensive.

Daniel frowned. "You've only known each other two weeks."

Hank put his arm around Beatrice in a protective manner. "Actually a bit more," he said. "I'd like to take Beatrice to New York to meet the rest of the family."

"We're leaving tomorrow," Beatrice put in. She smiled up at Hank in an unconsciously lovely way.

"And we'd like Carol to join us," Hank added.

"And Brittney, too." Beatrice smiled at her guest.

Brittney felt a lump in her throat. She'd thought Hank would be good for the other woman, but she had not envisioned this when she suggested Daniel invite the men to the house. Of course, she'd hoped some good would come of it, but marriage...

"Beatrice, this is too wonderful." Brittney rushed forward to hug the happy pair when Daniel stayed ominously silent. She cast a glance at him over her shoulder.

Daniel couldn't resist the combination plea and reprimand that Brittney gave him. Ignoring both his doubts and his sudden sense of relief, he held out a hand to Sanders. "Congratulations, Hank. You've got yourself a prize. Beatrice is a wonderful manager. She's kept me and Carol on track for years."

Brittney could have kissed him. His smile was warm, and his little speech just right. She gave him her brightest smile when he glanced her way. His mouth tilted into a sardonic grin.

"You'll just have to find yourself another manager," Hank said. His gaze also went to Brittney.

"Let's open some champagne to celebrate," Daniel suggested.

"Could we wait for Carol and Harry?" Beatrice asked. "I was so excited earlier, I forgot to eat. I'm hungry now. Would anyone like a sandwich and coffee?"

"I would," Hank immediately said.

Brittney and Daniel agreed they were hungry, too. Beatrice bustled out to the kitchen to prepare the food, Hank at her heels.

Daniel fetched ice and a silver bucket and put a bottle of champagne in to chill. After that, he leaned against the counter at the wet bar and watched Brittney.

"Happy?" he asked.

"For Hank and Beatrice? Yes."

"Was this what you planned when you had me invite him here?"

"Well, Beatrice was lonely. She needed someone." Brittney lifted her chin defiantly, as if she expected him to question this intuitive logic. He surprised her.

"Shall we make it a double announcement?"

Her hands flew to her throat to ease the thumping of her heart in that strange location. "By all means," she agreed, taking him up on the challenge in his eyes.

He laughed softly. "You won't back down an inch, will you?"

"You'll be the one to give in, Daniel. I only hope it won't be too late. I may change my mind, you know." She lifted the hair off her neck, then let it cascade down again.

A scowl crossed his brow. "I don't react well to threats."

"Tough. Life doesn't always consider our sensibilities."

He took a step toward her, but they were again interrupted, this time by the arrival of Carol and Harry. Carol was elated when she heard the news.

"Oh, Mums, this is wonderful," she exclaimed for the tenth time when they settled down to ham sandwiches, chips and drinks. "We'll have to go shopping while we're in New

York and get our dresses. What color are you going to wear? White?''

"Of course not—"

"Why not, if that's what you want?" Hank asked. "You'd look beautiful in a sack, of course, but you must please yourself in your choice, not society."

Beatrice gazed at him with her heart in her eyes. Brittney had to look away. She knew the feeling.

"We have other news," he continued. "We're going to bottle some of those great salad dressings Beatrice makes. I spoke to a friend who owns a food company, and he's going to open a line in her name."

"My mom, the salad-dressing tycoon!" Carol exclaimed, surprise and delight lighting her face. They all laughed.

Later, Brittney noticed that Daniel was quieter than usual, his mind obviously on other matters. Problems at work? she wondered. Or was he really upset by the other couple's news?

After they'd eaten, had the traditional toasts and quietened once more, he spoke up. "This is good timing. While you're gone, I'll do some traveling. I have to go north Friday. We're logging a new section, and I want to be on hand."

"Is there trouble?" Beatrice asked anxiously.

Daniel shook his head. "I want to make sure it's cut right. We're experimenting with leaving old forest next to sections of young trees in order to assess the growth patterns and to monitor the movements of animals."

"That sounds interesting," Brittney said.

"Brittney, what color dress would you like?" Carol turned to her mother. "You do want us in the wedding, don't you? Brittney and I'll be crushed if you don't." Without waiting for an answer, she rounded on Daniel.

"You will let us get something scrumptious, won't you, Daniel?"

"Whatever your heart desires," he assured her.

Carol gave a contented laugh. "I know the best shop in New York for wedding finery."

"I'm sure," Daniel said dryly. But he was smiling.

"I can't go to New York," Brittney quickly put in. "I have to find a place to live. Time's running out. I only have the rest of this week and next before I start work."

"Oh, you have to come," Carol wailed.

Brittney thought of her rapidly diminishing bankroll and shook her head. "When is the wedding to be?"

"Well, we haven't set a date." Beatrice looked at Hank.

"As soon as possible," he said firmly. "Before the end of the month."

That set everyone to talking and planning, except Brittney and Daniel. They remained silent. When the other two men finally left, Carol and Beatrice hurried upstairs to plan their wardrobe for the trip back east. Brittney helped Daniel take their glasses and plates to the kitchen. She put the dishes in the dishwasher while he rinsed them.

"Well, a whirlwind courtship," he mused, a slight smile on his hard mouth.

"You don't approve?"

"Yes. I think Hank will make Beatrice happy. He doesn't mind helping her with her decisions."

"He's so eager," she said wistfully. "It must be wonderful to be loved like that." She put the last glass in.

Hands on her shoulders spun her around before she could think. "Don't come on like Little Orphan Annie," he growled.

She shook her hair back from her face. "Maybe that's the way I feel. Only I don't want a Daddy Warbucks. I want—"

"Prince Charming to sweep you off your feet and carry you away to his castle where you'll live happily ever after." He spoke softly, but there was anger in his eyes. "Poor little kitten. No one to love."

His hands glided back to her shoulders. He caressed her with a kneading motion. She saw his eyes go to her mouth. His lips parted as if he were going to sample them. She felt her skin flush as his body moved against hers.

"I don't need your pity, Daniel," she said huskily, unable to stop her response to his blatant maleness.

"You won't get it. There are too many other things you make me feel."

"Like what?" she challenged.

He let her go. "Hot and bothered, to name one. Or is that two?" He laughed and held out a hand. "Come on, Cinderella. I'll walk you to your door."

"Will you come in?"

"You never let up on a guy, do you? You know you're wearing me down by degrees."

All kinds of fireworks erupted inside her. "Or maybe there's something in the air," she suggested coolly.

He stopped at her door and pressed her hand to his heart. "In here, kitten. You get me tied up into knots until even bondage sounds better than being tormented every hour of the day."

"It wouldn't be bondage, Daniel. Only the heady sweetness of fulfillment and lots of room to grow."

"And room to roam?"

"No." She was adamant. "You're not the type to take vows lightly. Neither am I. We'd be true to each other."

He sighed and eased back from her, obviously reluctant to leave her. "You're a temptation, I admit. All sweet woman and mine for the taking...almost."

She shook her head. "I won't hold you to marriage. When we make love, it'll be because we can't fight it any longer." She smiled up at him. "Because we find each other irresistible."

He pulled her into his arms, hard. "You shouldn't say things like that to a man. It drives him wild." He explored her back and sides, unable to hide the longing. "What am I going to do with you?" he muttered.

"Marry me," she said without being coy.

"I'm poor husband material. You'd regret your offer if I took you up on it."

"Then let me go."

"What?"

"Don't kiss me anymore. Don't look at me with your eyes all dark with passion. Don't let me know your body's reaction to mine. It's that simple, Daniel."

"Nothing's that simple," he growled.

Daniel tightened his hold on her as if someone were threatening to snatch her out of his arms. Dammit, she was driving him to the point that he didn't know what he wanted to do. Except rush her to his room and not let her out until he was completely sated with her, until the rage in his blood no longer pounded in his brain, until he was over this blind craving, once and for all.

"I bow to your greater experience," she said.

That made him angrier. "Don't try to be cynical. You can't carry it off."

She pushed against his chest, demanding to be free. "Go back to your usual women, Daniel. I don't want you."

He felt a strange pain in his midsection. "Since when?"

"You've convinced me you're not the man I thought you were."

She pulled away from him, leaving him standing in the hall, his arms emptied of her warmth. When he went to his room, it seemed empty, too.

What kind of man had she thought he was?

He paced from his bed to the window. Damn women, anyway. They got a man all heated up, then cut him down for reacting in the way nature intended. Blast! Who needed them? Not he. Not Daniel Montclair. He had better things to do. He had a business to run.

Maybe he'd go up north before Friday. One thing for sure: he wasn't staying here at the house with her.

Chapter Seven

"Yes, I understand. Of course, I'm disappointed. But these things happen. Yes. Please don't blame yourself. Really, I do understand. Thank you for calling. Goodbye."

Brittney hung up the phone. Well, so much for her job at the museum. The funding that was supposed to pay her salary hadn't been as much as the museum director had thought it would be. They could only afford part-time help. So she was back to job hunting.

It was a good thing she hadn't made a commitment on the tiny apartment she'd found yesterday. It had been a lovely place—two sunny rooms with a private entrance—in an older woman's home.

Well, she'd better call her grandfather and tell him the news. He'd probably insist that she come home. She unconsciously shook her head as she dialed the numbers to charge the call to her credit card. She didn't want to live with her grandfather. He tended to keep everyone under his thumb.

"Chapel residence," a familiar voice boomed into the room.

Brittney realized the speaker on the library phone was on and replaced the receiver. She adjusted the volume before she replied. "Hello, Stan."

"Brittney, good to hear from you," Stan exclaimed, warmth for her obvious in his deepened tone. His pleasure wrapped around her like a security blanket.

It suddenly felt good to be wanted just for herself, with no other complications. She realized how tense she'd been for three weeks. "It's lovely to speak to you, too. What are you doing at the house?"

"Discussing business with your grandfather. He was just directing me concerning your allowance."

Stan was the chief operations officer of her grandfather's many enterprises. He didn't usually handle small things such as her allowance. "Has the latest secretary quit?" she asked.

"I think so. She stormed out yesterday after telling him where to . . . ah . . . stuff the letter he was displeased with." There was a touch of resigned humor in Stan's voice.

"Well, she lasted six months. That's four more than the previous one." Brittney frowned even as she laughed with Stan. She might have to go home and take over.

"So, what's happening with you?"

"My job stopped before it got started," she said wryly. "I need my allowance extended until I find another." Her father had left her grandfather in control of the legacy until she was twenty-five. It stung her pride to have to ask for an extension.

The pause at the end of the line told her Stan was carefully thinking over what she'd said. "I know of a position here," he said, his manner light but not quite teasing. "Two, in fact. My house is pretty empty."

"Stan . . ." She rubbed a finger along the table edge, not wanting to hurt him.

"I know," he interrupted. "There's someone else. So, how are you doing with your heartthrob? No wedding yet?"

"If I ever get married, you'll be the first to know." Her laughter sounded hollow.

She became aware of someone in the room, moving behind her. She looked around, expecting Muggs. She encountered Daniel.

"Remember, I asked first," Stan said softly, seductively.

"I—I will," she stammered, picking up the receiver and flipping off the speaker. "Could I speak with Grandfather now?"

Without another glance, Daniel left the room.

"You bet," Stan said, his voice no longer filling the room with his friendly concern and banter.

After she explained her situation to her grandfather, she had to defend her reluctance to return to Stony River. "I need to prove I can make it on my own," she insisted.

"You haven't so far," her grandfather pointed out in his dry, aristocratic manner. "You have one more month, then I expect you to stop this nonsense and return to Stony River."

Another autocratic male who thought he knew what was best for her. She controlled her temper. "Thank you, Grandfather. I have to go now. Take care. I love you," she added.

There was a pause, then her grandfather said gruffly, "I love you, too. I wish you'd come home." He hung up.

She realized her hands were trembling when she replaced the receiver, just as they did after talking to her mother. Was she being unfair to her family? Sometimes she felt pulled in so many directions by the bonds of love.

It was the nature of children to go out and make a life of their own, she reminded herself. There was no way she could be what her mother or her grandfather wanted her to be— the dutiful daughter who did as told, and the constant buffer between them.

"Lunch is ready," Daniel said, appearing in the doorway.

Brittney rose and joined him. She noticed the stony glance he gave her. It seemed she had a knack for displeasing everyone these days. Tears filmed her eyes, but she refused to let them get the best of her.

Daniel watched Brittney's face as he pulled out a chair for her. Her eyes were overbright. Her hands shook slightly as she laid her napkin in her lap. As he recognized the signs of stress in her, he was sorry for his own abrupt anger.

It had been a stupid reaction anyway, he told himself. So some guy on the phone wanted to marry her. So what? She had probably had a dozen proposals by now.

He realized he felt possessive toward her, like a stag with one doe to protect. He also didn't like the fact that something about her conversation with her grandfather had upset her.

After Muggs served them a chilled salad with grilled shrimp and tiny hot rolls with a mouthwatering yeasty smell, he asked quietly, "Problems?"

She shook her head, not looking at him as she buttered a roll and took a bite. "Nothing serious." She smiled vaguely.

He didn't like the way she shut him out. "Did I hear you say the museum job didn't pan out?"

"You have good ears, Daniel."

He reddened at the twist to her smile that implied he'd been eavesdropping. "I was coming down the hall. The phone was on the speaker—I couldn't help but hear." His voice softened. "Is the job off?"

She nodded, then grimaced. "It's unbelievably difficult to find a position with a fine-arts degree."

"Secretaries are in great demand."

"I know. The counselor at school suggested that, so I found the museum job on my own. With Beatrice's help," she added.

Her face was composed. If he'd gone on the evidence of it alone, he'd have thought she wasn't disappointed, but he could see into her eyes. She was hurt.

Knowing that did strange things to him, things he didn't want to acknowledge. He'd noticed before that dealing with her family seemed to upset her. The loss of the job obviously added to her distress. It made him angry as well as protective, and he warned himself to back off.

"I might find something," he began, knowing he was crazy to suggest it. "The printing company always needs proofreaders."

She pushed her thick hair behind her shoulders. "That's kind of you, Daniel, but I can manage."

His fist clenched on his napkin. He forced it to relax. There was nothing to get upset about. He'd offered. She'd refused. It was plain she could handle her own affairs. She didn't need him.

That fact should have brought him instant relief. Instead it increased his temper. Carol and Beatrice had no qualms about asking for help. What made Brittney so damned proud?

"I didn't mean to make you angry by refusing your offer," she said, reading his reaction. "It's just—" she shrugged her shoulders "—I don't really need any favors."

He felt a flush rise in his cheeks. "It wasn't a favor," he practically growled. He forced himself to hold on to his temper. He was only making things worse for her. He wanted to go out and slay dragons or something—anything to erase the hurt.

Bah! Women always used a man's instincts against him. They had honed that skill to an art. He knew which was the craftier sex, if not the stronger.

"So, what are you doing here?" she asked brightly, obviously putting her cares aside. "I figured you'd be in the north woods by now."

"I came by to pick up some clothes I'll need." He turned away. Her smile was so damned sweet.

"Your lumberjack outfit?" she teased.

"Yeah. Do you want to go up with me?"

He was almost as surprised as she was by the invitation. "Up north?"

"Yes. I have a cabin by a little creek. You might enjoy it."

She bit her bottom lip nervously, almost wringing a groan from him. He wanted to kiss her. It had been three days, and he was starving for the taste of her.

Hell, if it was this bad now, what was he going to do if she went up to the cabin?

"We can drive up first thing in the morning," he heard himself say, coaxing her to agree.

Brittney thought of the emptiness of the past three days without him. It would be insane to say yes. She knew that...just as she knew she was most likely going to do just that.

"If you're looking for a tactful way to refuse, don't bother. Simply say no," he said.

"It sounds interesting." She tried for a lighter mood. "But I can't figure out why you asked."

He chuckled, sending a shiver down her back. "Neither can I. It's asking for trouble, but then, I've always been a fool for a dare. You're a challenge I can't resist."

His narrowed gaze taunted her with memories of their mutual passion. He'd told her—and shown her—more than once that he was susceptible to her. If she went to the cabin, was she agreeing to stay with him in the intimate sense?

After the disappointment about the museum and the small but meaningful confrontation with her grandfather, she knew she was vulnerable to Daniel's strength. She wanted to rest in his arms and let him soothe away the knocks and bruises of the world, to have him kiss her and make everything all right.

"Nothing will happen," he said after a lengthy pause.

"Won't it?" Her laughter was shaky.

"I won't take advantage of you."

It was a promise that brought its own pain. "Daniel, the honorable man," she said.

He shrugged. "Perhaps. But where you're concerned, don't trust me too much, kitten. I'd like to eat you in one bite."

They ate the rest of their lunch in silence. When he finished, he wiped his mouth and tossed the napkin down. "I've got to go back to the office. I'll spend the night here. We leave at the crack of dawn. I want to be on the road by five or so."

She stared after him when he left. It seemed the decision had been taken out of her hands, and she spent the afternoon trying to decide if she was happy about it.

"Did you bring sturdy shoes?" Daniel asked, taking his eyes from the highway to glance at her sandaled foot.

"Yes. I have a pair of boots and some jogging shoes."

"You'll need a jacket."

"I have one. And a hooded sweatshirt."

He nodded and kept his eyes on I-35. After a while, he turned on the radio, and they listened to soft rock. He stopped for a quick coffee break at the exit to Highway 53. Then they drove farther north and across the Mesabi Iron Range. The road grew rougher.

Shortly before ten, he turned off the main road and headed west. The county road was paved, but was rougher and narrower than the ones they'd been traveling. He turned northwest onto a gravel lane. They arrived at their destination just when the gravel gave out and a one-lane dirt road started.

He pulled to a stop under a carport next to a rustic cabin. It looked tiny. Very tiny.

Daniel got both their bags out of the back of the Blazer and carried them to the front door. Brittney followed, toting her purse and cosmetic case with a strap over each shoulder.

"It looks...charming," she said. Could it possibly have more than one bedroom?

Daniel opened the door and let her go in first. She darted a quick look around the small living room. A fireplace dominated the wall next to the door. She saw two bedrooms, one off each side of the living room. The kitchen, with a big round table, was at the back of the house. A tiny bathroom with a shower opened off one side of it. A storage room was on the other side.

"The bedroom to the right has its own door into the bathroom, so you don't have to go through the living room and kitchen to get to it. I think of it as the guest room." Crossing behind her, he led the way.

"Oh. Thank you." She went in and laid her stuff on a rocking chair. A quilt of bright squares covered the twin bed. A wool blanket lay on a cedar chest at the end. A small dresser and night table made up the rest of the furniture. Looking at the small bed, she had visions that tightened every muscle in her body.

"You can relax. I know I said I wanted to eat you in one bite yesterday, but I'll behave."

He was rather grim and had been the entire trip. If he disliked her presence so much, he shouldn't have invited her, she decided. Having recovered her equilibrium from the day before, she could laugh at life again. "Darn," she muttered.

He dropped her bag on the chest. "But not," he warned, "if you keep that up." His eyes never left her mouth as he bent closer and closer.

Her lips parted, ready for his kiss.

He walked to the door. "Play fair," he said huskily. "If I have to behave, you have to, too."

"Okay."

After he strode out, she put her clothes in the drawers. Having no idea how long they would be here, she had brought enough for a week. Finished, she changed to jeans, a shirt and an old pair of jogging shoes.

"I'm ready to see your logging operations," she called, going into the living room.

Daniel was in the kitchen. "Right. Let me see what we have for dinner." He rummaged through the refrigerator, checking various packages. "Are you hungry?"

"No. Are you?"

He looked over his shoulder. "Don't ask leading questions." He slammed the refrigerator door. "We'll have lunch at the camp. Come on. Bring a jacket. It may be dark before we get back."

She followed his orders and joined him again in the truck. "Who takes care of your place and buys your groceries?" she asked when they were off bouncing along a logging trail.

"The cook's wife."

"Oh."

She felt suddenly foolish for asking.

The sardonic lift of his eyebrow indicated he suspected her train of thought. "Jealous?" he inquired with a hard glance.

"Don't let it go to your head," she remarked, refusing to say anything more.

"Now you know how I felt when I heard that guy remind you he'd proposed to you first."

"Jealous?" she said, astounded.

"Don't let it go to your head."

He swung the wheel and gunned the motor as they climbed a steep ridge, zigzagging along the one-lane road. Her thoughts ran along similar paths, back and forth but getting nowhere. She gave up and let the questions fade.

Daniel was attracted. He'd made no secret of his desire. But that was all he wanted from her. He'd made that clear, too. It was disheartening. Her prospects didn't look too bright at present; careerwise or heartwise.

"I can almost hear the wheels turning," he remarked, reaching over and tapping her temple.

She laughed. "Do you need a secretary or proofreader up here? I would take either. I love the forest. It smells wonderful. And the quiet seeps right into your soul."

He wasn't fooled. "Good. Maybe you won't brood while you're here. Life often has a silver lining, Brittney."

His unexpected encouragement caught her off guard. Before she could answer, they were at the logging camp. Men were everywhere, busy as ants at a sugar mill. Only in this case they were moving logs that were a hundred feet long or more.

"Horses!" she cried in surprise. A team of two huge beasts pulled a log into the clearing and stopped.

"They can get into tight places," Daniel explained. He climbed out and came around to open the door for her.

She jumped down.

Taking her arm, he led her around the camp, explaining what was happening. "That's a come-along." He pointed to a chain and harness fastened around the log as they passed the horses. Daniel spoke to the man who guided them.

Brittney saw the man look at her with interest in his eyes. He was movie-star handsome, she noted. Probably had a mass of broken hearts within a twenty-mile radius.

"I'm Paul," he called to her when Daniel failed to introduce them. His grin was infectious.

"I'm Brittney Cha—"

"She's spoken for," Daniel interrupted. The steel in his eyes warned off the younger man.

"Daniel, that was terrible," she scolded when he ushered her toward a large tent. "I am not spoken for."

"Up here, you are." He pivoted to face her, his expression harsh. "Up here, you're my woman. Don't forget it, or I'll remind you in the only way I know how."

"How?" she demanded, tossing the challenge right back at him. He wasn't going to be as autocratic with her as her family was.

He didn't hesitate. Wrapping one arm around her and taking her chin in one hand, he brought her lips up so he could crush them under his mouth.

Brittney had expected the kiss to be hard, but it was soft. She had expected fury; she got gentleness.

Tears burned her eyes at the sweetness of it.

The kiss was brief, but it was enough to be noticed. The men hooted and yelled advice to the boss.

"Hey, boss, do we get turns? I'd give a month's wages," Paul called to them.

"No turns," Daniel said, starting for the tent once more. "Like I said, the lady's spoken for." In an aside, he murmured, "Any objections?" His eyes dared her to have any.

Brittney shook her head, too stunned to speak. This was what it would be like to be his woman, she realized. This was how it would feel to be loved completely by him. He wouldn't hide his feelings. He was a man brave enough to show the world his heart. It was the way she'd dreamed of being loved.

Shaken, she followed him silently into the huge canvas tent. Inside she found long tables and many chairs. A man worked at a range at one end. "This is the dining hall?" she asked.

"Yeah. Sam, how soon until lunch?" Daniel called to the short, wiry man who was pouring corn-bread batter into a large skillet. The skillet looked too heavy to pick up. The cook grabbed it with one hand and flung it into the oven.

He turned with a grin on his thin, lined face. "Forty minutes. I didn't expect you today. Shoulda known you'd show up. Never fails when we're having fried chicken and corn bread." He winked at Brittney as if they shared a joke at Daniel's expense.

Brittney thought of the fancy dishes Beatrice had Mrs. Muggs prepare. "Now I know why you like to come up here," she declared.

"Sam, this bossy female is Brittney. You two should get along real fine. She's as stubborn as you are and as sharp-tongued."

Sam wiped his hands on the white apron he wore. "I can tell she's like me—sweet as an angel. Right, honey?"

"Right, Sam. I'm glad to meet you. I think I might need an ally while I'm here."

Daniel dropped an arm around her waist and pulled her close. "I'm the boss. Don't either of you forget it."

His easy teasing set the tone for the meal. The men were comfortable around Daniel. Brittney could see the respect

in their manner and hear their liking in their remarks. She
hadn't laughed so much in a long time.

Perhaps that was why the entrance of a woman—not just
a woman, but a gorgeous one—knocked her for a loop. She
had let her defenses down and was unprepared.

"Hey, Dinah," Paul cried out, "is there anyone *finah*
back where you come from?"

"I'm the last of the breed, Paul," she said, taking a tray
and filling a plate to almost the same proportions as the
men.

"A woman lumberjack?" Brittney asked, still staring.

A sinking feeling hit the pit of her stomach. Dinah, as-
suming that was her name, was tall and willowy. Her pants,
a pair of faded brown cords, were old and fitted like a glove.
Her figure was perfect. So was her face. As was the mane of
black curly hair and the dark eyes that shone like obsidian.

"A botanist," Daniel explained, moving over to make
room for the woman at their table. "Dinah works for the
state. Part of the timber we cut is state forest."

"I see," Brittney said, not seeing at all. She suddenly felt
very unsure of her place in the scheme of things.

He stood, a smile on his handsome face as he welcomed
the female botanist. "Glad you could join us," he said.
"Dinah, this is a family friend, Brittney Chapel. Brittney,
Dinah St. Cloud."

The women said hello together. Brittney hoped that her
smile was not as stiff as it felt.

"Are you staying long?" Dinah inquired, picking up her
fork.

Was the woman hoping to get rid of her? Brittney wondered, stung by the question. "I don't know. That's up to
Daniel."

Oh, heavens, was that a catty reply or wasn't it? Brittney
groaned to herself. She had no right to the possessive feel-

ings she was experiencing. Daniel could have a woman behind every tree as far as she was concerned.

And if they all showed up while she was here, she'd kill
him!

She felt his hand on her thigh under the table. He gave her
leg a squeeze, then said to the beautiful botanist, "I thought
I'd stay and see how the cutting went in the new section.
Brittney and I'll be here for about a week."

His hand moved up and down, then rested above her
knee. He made soothing motions. She reached down as casually as she could and removed it, placing his hand on his
own leg. He immediately moved it back.

She realized there was no way she could restrain him
without causing a scene. She certainly wasn't going to do
that in front of Miss Eagle-Eye Botanist—Dinah whatever-
her-name-was.

Brittney lost her appetite while Dinah ate with gusto.

"Umm, that was good. You have the best grub of the line
kitchens. Sam, when you want to leave your wife and this
slave driver, let me know. I'd marry you in a minute."

"I'm thinking of taking cooking lessons," Paul declared.

"You'll never be as good as Sam here in a hundred
years." Dinah laughed at Paul's wail of outrage, then finished her meal.

If she had to eat like a lumberjack, the least she could do
was look like one, Brittney thought grumpily. She deter-
minedly held Daniel's hand to keep him from driving her
crazy with his little touches under the table. When she
glanced at him, he was smiling.

No, he was laughing, she realized, looking into his eyes
more closely. At her. Embarrassed and furious, she stood
abruptly. Everyone stopped and looked at her.

"I...uh, I'm tired. I think I'll go...walk back to the cabin. To get the kinks out. It was nice meeting you all." Her eyes took in the thirty or forty men as well as Dinah. Nodding with as much grace as she could muster, she went out, leaving Daniel at the table with the female Paul Bunyan.

Daniel caught up with her before she reached the Blazer. He took her shoulders and pushed her against the door of the truck and held her trapped there, his body close so that she felt his warmth.

"I've known Dinah since she was a kid. She's an old friend."

Brittney met his gaze bravely. "I'm aware of the fact that I made a complete fool of myself. You don't have to explain your relationship to me."

He grinned. "I think I like your being on edge. Now you know how I feel when men stop dead in their tracks when you're around."

"They don't," she protested.

"Like hell." He was suddenly much closer. "Paul nearly burst his britches when he got a look at you."

"He flirts with everybody, including your old friend."

"There was a scramble among the men to see who could get to our table first. Didn't you notice?" His mouth hovered above hers.

"No." She looked over his shoulder, staring into the trees. "Let me go, Daniel. Someone might see and think you really mean this the way it looks."

"Like Dinah?" he asked softly. "I don't care."

His mouth brushed hers, a slow caress that confused her as much as his words. Was he just protecting her from any advances the rough and rowdy men might make if they thought she was free?

"Daniel."

She got no further. His mouth took hers. It was a hungry kiss. It told her of his need, suppressed for days while he'd stayed away from the house.

She reminded herself he'd only invited her here because he'd overheard her woes and felt sorry for her. Desire didn't mean anything permanent. Neither did his protectiveness. Daniel was naturally solicitous of everyone in his care.

His tongue glided over her mouth, and she forgot every argument about holding him at arm's length. She wrapped her arms around his neck and held on for dear life. With each movement of his lips on hers, of his tongue against hers, she was propelled into a maelstrom of need as great as his.

He leaned into her, curving his hard body to fit hers. Her breasts responded urgently, wanting his touch. She remembered how he had caressed them and teased them into peaks. She wanted him to do that again.

Finally, he eased the kiss and permitted space between them. "If we keep this up, all my resolutions about this week are going to go up in smoke."

"So, why should you be any different from me?" she murmured awkwardly.

He laughed at her quip, delivered in a light but shaken tone. "One of us has to be sensible."

She climbed into the truck when he moved her aside and opened the door. "Why?" she asked from the relative safety inside.

After climbing in, he rested one arm on the steering wheel and turned to her. He studied her face in a restless manner. "Because." At her stubborn expression, he added, "I'm not going to fall into the marriage trap—not even for your sweet kisses, Brittney. I'd hate it and resent you for it in no time."

Brittney averted her gaze as he turned on the ignition and started the truck. "No apologies, Daniel. I'm a big girl. I can face the facts."

"I know. Lately, I've begun to realize what a lot of courage you have. It can't be easy to go against your family."

She started to deny his statement, then she realized she didn't have to. He understood. "My mother and grandfather don't see why I need to work. They want me to marry and produce the next heir. It's my duty. That's the one thing they agree on."

His hands tightened on the wheel. "Have they picked out the man, too?"

"My grandfather wants me to marry Stan. My mother wants me to marry the cousin of the governor of Louisiana, who works with my brother."

"But you want to marry me," he added softly. "Am I part of your rebellion against them?"

She smiled ruefully. "No. You're part of an obsession, one that I'm convinced isn't good for me at all."

They arrived back at the cabin. He didn't get out. "I need to check on some things with Dinah. Why don't you rest? I'll see you later, say around five?"

She nodded and climbed down.

He didn't drive off until she was in the cabin with the door closed behind her. Tired, she went to the bedroom, kicked off her shoes and lay on the quilt. She drifted asleep thinking of Daniel and Dinah and wondering if they'd been lovers.

Chapter Eight

Brittney rested for an hour, then decided to walk up to the camp. It was no more than a mile. She'd seen a big platter of cookies on the side table, and she was hungry now. She put on her shoes, smoothed the quilt and left. On the way, she had a talk with herself about jealousy.

She remembered reading that jealousy sprang from low self-worth or a sense of insecurity. She knew hers stemmed from the latter. She was in love with Daniel; he wasn't in love with her.

So maybe it was time to move on.

She'd given it the ol' college try. She'd set her goal and gone for it, blatantly, just the way Carol would have. But it hadn't worked. One part of valor was knowing when to quit. She thought that time had come.

For a moment tears burned her eyes. She rubbed them away, determined not to cry over what was not to be.

The campsite was quiet when she arrived twenty minutes later. The activity had moved deeper into the forest, judging from the noise of chain saws and the low roar of equipment. A partially loaded logging truck was parked to one side. Paul's big Belgians cropped the sparse grass in a clearing.

She ducked under the flap of the dining tent. Paul and Sam, the cook, were sitting at a table, hands cupped around coffee mugs.

"Well, look who's here," Paul drawled, his eyes running over her conformation like a judge's at a horse show.

She wrinkled her nose at him, then smiled at Sam. "How does one get a cup of coffee and one of those big chocolate-chip cookies I saw in here earlier?"

"Just ask," Sam replied. He peered toward the opening. "Did you walk up?"

"Yes. Daniel had some work to do. I took a nap—"

"And Daniel left you all alone?" Paul rolled his eyes in disbelief. "Somebody better talk to that boy." He grinned at her.

Sam tossed Paul a hard glance. "Better let Daniel do his own talking," he advised. "Coffee's over here, cookies under that cover," he said to Brittney. "Help yourself. It's there twenty-four hours a day."

"Thanks." She found the mugs on a table beside a huge coffee urn. The cookies were beside it in a plastic container. She selected one, then added another after deciding she was very hungry. She returned to the table and sat beside Sam.

"I'd better check the coffee," he decided. He looked in the pot, then headed for the stove at the back of the tent.

"Twenty-four hours?" she questioned. "Do the men work night and day?"

"Mostly from sunup to sundown," Paul answered. "The season is short for logging. When the snow comes, we shut down."

"I see. Have you found any logs with spikes?"

Paul propped his chin on his fists and studied her for a minute. "No. Worried about Daniel?" He looked sympathetic. "You have it bad for him, huh?"

She felt terribly vulnerable all at once, as if everyone could see into her heart. She shook back her hair in a carefree way and laughed. "Now that would be telling," she scolded, adopting his playful manner.

He reached over and pulled a lock of her hair in a friendly fashion. "Daniel can be pretty tough. If you need a friend, you can call on me."

There was understanding in his eyes, as if he'd had experience with women who'd tangled with Daniel and gotten hurt. Perhaps he'd supplied a comforting shoulder for Dinah? "Thanks," she said with a lightness she didn't feel. "I'll put you on my list."

"Great. Sam's made fresh coffee. Let's have some and raid the cookie jar again."

They refilled their cups and nabbed two more cookies each. For the next hour, they laughed and talked. Paul told her about the logging operations. She learned he was an agriculture consultant and expert on nonchemical farming. He wrote books and articles on the subject. He also had an experimental farm that bordered on state forest.

"The Montclairs have been tree farming here for generations with no problems. They've never cut more than the land can replenish, so they have an endless cycle of renewable resource, and Daniel is willing to experiment in order to do a better job."

Brittney tried but failed to stifle the warm glow she felt upon hearing approval of Daniel.

"I'm supervising some trials with old and new growth for him. Dinah is in control of the state's interest."

"So you and she work together," Brittney mused.

He shrugged. "Dinah doesn't work with anyone. She rules her domain with an iron hand, and woe to anyone who gets in her way."

Brittney detected undercurrents of dislike. She smiled. The gorgeous botanist probably hadn't fallen for Paul's charm. Brittney found him easy company; he didn't really expect her to take his teasing seriously.

Suddenly the tent flap was raised and Daniel stepped in. His eyes flicked over the room until they lighted on her. He strode over and glared at Paul. "Don't your horses need tending?"

Paul stood without haste. "Maybe."

"I suggest you see to them."

"The thing about working with horses, fillies and such," Paul drawled, hooking his thumbs in his belt, "is you have to be easy around them, else they're liable to run off." He tipped his head to Brittney. "See you." He ambled out.

Brittney stared after him, then back at Daniel. The conversation made no sense, but she didn't need second sight to recognize the anger in Daniel's eyes. What had she done now?

"Don't you ever leave the house without letting me know," he said, his jaw rigid.

Brittney had never liked being trounced on, but she held her temper in line. "How was I supposed to do that? I had no idea where you were." She kept her tone reasonable.

"You should have stayed until I came for you." He stomped over to the coffeepot, filled a mug and brought it back to the table. Brittney noticed that Sam had disappeared.

"I don't report in, Daniel." She spoke very calmly.

He took a slug of coffee and burnt his tongue. "Hellfire—"

Brittney managed to straighten her face when he cast a furious glance her way.

"This is dangerous country." He took up his quarrel with her again. "How was I supposed to know where you'd gone? You could have gotten lost. You could have been eaten by a bear. I don't want you going off like that again. And another thing, stay away from the men. I will not have them rattled by your flirting."

"Flirting!"

"They work with saws and axes. I don't want someone losing a foot because he was mooning over you."

He crossed his arms over his chest and stared down at her—an outraged, imperious male bent on having his say.

Brittney's temper frayed to the snapping point. "And I suppose it doesn't bother them to have that amazon of the forest prancing around them all day?" she snarled, slamming her own mug down and splashing coffee on the table.

Daniel looked dumbfounded. "Who?"

"Don't pretend you don't know. Dinah somebody, the botanist with the great figure, curly black hair and eyes to drown in."

"Dinah St. Cloud." He supplied the name. His eyebrows drew together as his frown deepened. "She at least has enough sense not to go wandering off in the woods. I don't have to worry about calling out a search party—"

"Search party! For heaven's sake, I only walked a mile up a well-traveled road. Really, Daniel, this is ridiculous."

Daniel opened his mouth, then closed it. She was right. It was ridiculous to be standing there yelling insults across the table at each other. But when he'd arrived at the cabin and she had been gone... Then to find her laughing and fluttering those gorgeous lashes at a man who slayed women with just a smile... Dammit, it had been too much.

"Try to have some consideration for other people," he finally muttered, and stalked out, leaving her there with her mouth open.

"I always think of other people," she yelled after him. "It's been one of the biggest problems of my life, and I'm not going to do it anymore."

The roaring departure of a truck was the only answer.

"He's gone," Sam said, coming in the back flap. "Whew, he sure was mad." He looked at her with new respect. "Course, you were, too. Sounded like two bobcats in here."

"I know," she said unhappily. She wiped up the coffee spill, noticing that Daniel hadn't had but the one swallow of his coffee. "Can I help you with dinner? I don't feel like going to the cabin right now."

Sam set her to work peeling about a hundred potatoes. She discovered he had an assistant, a plump Oriental man, who nodded when introduced, then got right to work. Brittney forgot her anger, in awe of the mountain of food being prepared.

"How many are we cooking for?" she asked.

"Thirty-six, give or take three or four."

It was dark before all the men came in. She heard the sounds of running water as they showered. A generator supplied power for the pump that brought water from the creek.

When they congregated for the meal, she wondered uneasily what she was supposed to do. Daniel wasn't with them. Well, she would eat, then if he hadn't appeared, she'd ask somebody to drive her back to the cabin. That seemed fair.

Just as she sat down between two stocky lumberjacks, he walked in. There was a moment of silence in the tent, then the men resumed their dinner. Daniel filled a plate and brought it over to the table where she sat. A space appeared as if by magic beside her.

With the ease of long practice, he began a conversation with the men about the day's work. Soon they were all talking and joking normally again. Brittney donned a pleasant expression but didn't join in. She was aware of Daniel with every atom of her being. His casual glances made her decidedly nervous.

She could feel the force of a storm gathering like clouds on the horizon. He was still angry with her, she surmised, then shifted uncomfortably in her chair at the prospect of spending the evening with him in his tiny cabin.

As it turned out, nothing happened. He told her goodnight and went into his bedroom and closed the door. That was all.

The week continued in the same fashion. He spent many hours with Paul and Dinah, planning the fall planting program. Brittney had known Daniel loved the woods, but she hadn't realized how much until now. This was where he belonged.

Toward her, he maintained a distant coolness, acting the polite host and no more. Never did he give in to the desire she sometimes witnessed in his eyes.

It is the way of all things, she mused. Some gained their dreams, others didn't. Obviously she wasn't to be one of the lucky ones. So be it. She'd get on with her life. She had things to do—like find a job and a place to live.

They returned to the lake house on Friday. Carol and Beatrice had arrived the day before. They were already on the phone to caterers, florists and the minister, making arrangements for the wedding.

"We have only two weeks from Sunday to get all this set up," Beatrice reminded them worriedly. "I'm almost afraid to call anyone today. It's Friday the thirteenth."

Daniel was not quite as patient as usual about Beatrice's anxieties. He bluntly assured her everything would turn out fine. When she still fretted, he managed a tight smile and told her he'd order up a sunny day with no clouds or flies to mar the scene.

Brittney almost believed he could. During the evening meal, he approved all the wedding plans. He bid them goodnight and left right after the dessert.

"We won't see any more of him until it's time to walk down the aisle," Carol predicted.

Daniel poured a cup of coffee and returned to the large desk that occupied a corner of his bedroom. After a few minutes of reading, he got up and turned on the radio to a mellow FM station. The silence nagged at him.

That wasn't all, he admitted with a restless sigh. Brittney was a mischievous spirit bent on tormenting him until he joined her.

Just thinking about her brought on an eager response from his body. He was already throbbing with need. He frowned impatiently. This was totally out of control.

She had intruded into every aspect of his life—even here, in his personal sanctuary. Just two days ago, he'd lost track of the conversation in a meeting with his banker and the company finance officer because something had reminded him of *her*.

The old out-of-sight-out-of-mind adage wasn't working at all. He still wanted her, thought of her, dreamed of her.

And the only way he could have her was through marriage, no matter what she said about not holding him to that if they ever did make love in a moment of mutual madness.

Marriage. As if he didn't have enough demands on his time. Since he'd taken over the family enterprises, he'd rarely had a minute to himself. Except when he went to the cabin in the woods. Then he was his own man.

No woman...no *wife* would give a man the space he needed to breathe freely once in a while. The women he knew had never understood his need to be alone. And most women hated the woods. Oh, yeah, they were all sweetness and light before marriage. But afterward? Just let a man suggest roughing it in a log cabin and see what kind of response he got. Beatrice had let Adam know quickly enough that the north country was not her favorite place.

Of course, Brittney had seemed to enjoy herself up there. She was a person who knew when to be quiet. He brought his thoughts to a halt with a curse. There she was, intruding again!

He rubbed a hand wearily across his eyes. Sometimes even marriage didn't sound half bad—

He abruptly thrust the chair back and stood. No way. It wouldn't work; everyone knew that after marriage came divorce.

His frown became ferocious. Divorce was out, especially if they had kids. He'd not have his grow up in a broken home, shuffled from one parent to another—

Wait a minute. He wasn't going to have kids. He wasn't going to get a divorce. He wasn't even going to get married!

What he *was* going to do was quit thinking of that vamp in kitten's clothing, he vowed.

He forced himself away from the window and the moonlight. Back at the desk, he went over the accountant's figures once more before he went to bed. Tomorrow night he'd see Brittney at the party the Rostaners were throwing for

Beatrice and Hank. It had been a week since he'd left her at the house.

He groaned then, realizing he'd already broken his vow.

Brittney smiled and spoke to guests at the party honoring Beatrice and Hank. The happy couple and their hosts were standing at the door, welcoming most of the people who lived around the lake to the gala event. Reporters from two papers were there.

Daniel was somewhere in the crowd. She'd said hello to him earlier. He'd returned her greeting, given her one of his hell-frozen-over glances, then holed up in a corner with a business acquaintance. It was a good thing she'd gotten over her foolish notions about them.

"Hi. Can I get you something cool to drink?" Ed Zimm touched her on the shoulder, then took her hand and squeezed it.

"That would be lovely." She removed her hand while returning his smile. "Oh, here comes the waiter now."

They helped themselves to tall glasses of punch from the tray.

"So, how's it going? Find a place yet?"

She shook her head. "I need a job first. The museum didn't work out. They ran out of money."

Ed's laughter was sympathetic, his manners charming. A person could have fun with him without getting involved.

"I'm going to look at some property north of town tomorrow. Would you like to join me?"

She wanted to say yes, but something held her back. Ed was an experienced man of the world. If she started seeing him, he'd soon expect more than she wanted to give—unlike Daniel, who had refused to take what she'd so blatantly offered.

Really, she had to stop thinking about him and comparing all other men to him. He wasn't Mr. Wonderful, she reminded herself. Daniel had a few warts, just like other mortals.

"We could make it a day," Ed continued. "I know a neat little place where we could have dinner. Do you like Italian?"

"Pasta is a major weakness of mine," she admitted.

A hand settled on the back of her neck. "Good," a deep voice said. "I'll let you do the cooking."

Brittney stared at Daniel. He smiled at her so intimately she felt a blush start up her face. "W-what?"

"Sorry, she's going to be busy," he said to Ed. "Will you excuse us? I need to talk to Brittney about a family matter."

She allowed herself to be led away... only to prevent a scene, she told herself. Daniel had a dangerous gleam in his eye.

"What do you need to talk about?" she asked, trying subtly to halt their progress toward a French door. It was useless.

He whisked her outside and closed the door behind them. The last thing Brittney saw was Carol's grin as she waved to her over Harry's shoulder.

Daniel took her arm, more gently this time, and urged her to a path through the rose garden. He evidently knew where he was going because they soon came to a swing hidden in a little alcove covered with a flowering vine. He wiped the bench with his handkerchief before indicating she should be seated.

She carefully arranged the deep red silk of her evening dress around her, as if it were the most important task in the world. At last, when he didn't speak but stood there looking down at her with the moonlight pouring over them, she asked, "What family matter do we need to discuss?"

He gave a short laugh. "Damned if I know."

She stood, anger sprouting like thistle seeds inside her. Instead of giving rein to it, she tilted her head and looked up at her handsome escort. "I think you just wanted to get me alone," she reprimanded, trying for a light note.

He shifted restlessly, as if his dinner jacket constricted his movements. "I wanted to get you away from Ed," he admitted.

"Why?"

He reached for her then. "Because I want you for myself."

She heard the irony, saw it in his slight smile before he kissed her.

His kiss was strangely subdued, as if she were a piece of crystal, and so gentle it caused an ache in her. He caressed her with both hands on her cheeks, rubbing the skin tenderly while his lips ravished her mouth with a hunger she sensed more than felt.

It didn't last long enough. Heaven never does. She laid her head on his chest when the kiss ended. He began to dance with her, moving with her over the level ground while stars reeled in her eyes like drunken fireflies.

She realized she was near tears and that her control wasn't as firm as she'd like it to be. For one thing, she was tired. Helping Beatrice with her wedding was a taxing job. The older woman needed support in every decision.

For another, the emotional wear of being around Daniel was taking its toll. He wanted her, he was jealous of other men, but he didn't want involvement. There were no signs that he was beginning to realize he couldn't live without her, that the joy of being with her was greater than the dislike of being further entangled in the responsibilities and demands of family life. The push and pull of their relationship was suddenly too much.

After the wedding she'd return to Shreveport. She'd visit with her grandfather and look for a job. Maybe she'd take over the secretarial duties until he found someone who'd put up with his demanding ways.

This would probably be the last time she'd be in Daniel's arms, she realized. Ignoring the ache inside, she closed her eyes and gave herself to the night and the music drifting on the night air from the party. Daniel and moonlight. She'd never forget this moment.

"Aren't you going to recite the advantages of marriage to me tonight?" he asked abruptly.

She didn't say anything for a minute, but just looked at him, the moonlight casting his features in silver shadows.

Daniel smiled when she stopped dancing and stared at him. He'd caught her by surprise. Good. That was the way she affected him each time he saw her—surprised, as if he had thought the hunger for her should have faded. Instead, it gnawed at him.

"Companionship," she said at last.

Her answer caught him off guard. It was spoken softly, with none of the playful challenge of the past month. He thought of his apartment, empty and silent. He thought of the cabin, filled with her quiet ways during the week they'd spent up there. They'd shared laughter and conversation as well as the finely drawn tension of desire. Companionship could be nice.

"I can get that whenever I want it," he reminded her. "When I want the freedom of male company, I head up north. When I want female friends, I pick up the phone."

"Droves of them at your beck and call, I would imagine," she agreed. A smile flickered over her mouth and was gone. He didn't understand her mood.

He thought of the loneliness of the past week and all the women he *hadn't* called. "Yeah."

"But those are cursory affairs, Daniel," she said, suddenly earnest, as if she were trying to convince a friend to do something for his health, such as quit smoking. "There's no depth, no meaning. A wife shares life with you. She runs your home, plans your social activities and helps you enjoy life."

"The feminine touch, huh?"

He tightened his arms around her and started dancing again as he envisioned all the ways she might touch him. Funny, no other woman's touch appealed to him. She'd probably laugh if she knew just how long it had been since he'd enjoyed another woman's caress in the intimate sense.

"Yes." She leaned back against his arms so that her throat was tantalizingly exposed to his gaze.

He bent and kissed her there before he could stop himself. All this talk about the benefits of marriage was a waste of time. He had only thought to taunt her a bit for flirting with Ed.

Was he jealous?

Damned right. She wasn't going to get involved with a womanizer like that. If she wanted to experiment with her sensuality, then it was going to be with him. It was natural for her to be curious about what she was missing, he admitted.

Feeling protective and somewhat noble, he asked, "What else?"

"Together, a husband and wife establish a home—the oldest, most stable unit of civilization in the world."

"Which a man pays for."

"Lots of women work nowadays," she chided. "They take on two careers when they marry, a third if they have children."

He was suddenly swamped with pictures: coming home at the end of the day, Brittney there waiting, her arms open, her lips ready for his kiss, her body ready for his . . .

An ache grew in him, not just of lust, but of other needs he couldn't define. She had a stubborn streak a mile wide, she was fiercely independent, yet she was the most feminine woman he'd ever met—sexy and caring and funny and gentle.

"Do you want children?" he murmured.

"Yes, children are an advantage of marriage."

She gazed into the distance as if she envisioned the children she and her husband would someday have. Daniel felt a tightness invade his throat. She would have beautiful children.

"They add their own specialness to life," she continued. "A bridge to the future stretching back through you and your parents, and on and on."

"And there's the pleasure of creating them," he added harshly, cynically. "That's how you women trap men."

She ignored his barb. "Marriage brings many pleasures, I think. Certainly there's sex, but there's also the emotional fulfillment that comes from sharing the good things in life. Don't you think so?" Her tone changed, becoming playful and challenging.

"Yes." He breathed in the fragrance of her perfume, imagining all the places she put it. He'd like to discover them, each one, one by one by one. . . .

"And they'd be there for each other in the bad times, too—like you were there for Beatrice and Carol when your brother died."

He remembered the grief. Having responsibility had helped him over his. Life had demanded so much of his attention, he'd never had time to become maudlin. But he'd disliked those demands. He'd envisioned a different life for himself. He'd wanted to roam, to discover the world. Instead, he rarely got out of Minnesota.

"And of course, it's nice to have someone to cuddle up to on cold Minnesota nights," she added on a brighter note. "Three hundred and sixty-five nights a year, Daniel."

The sweet, seductive murmur of her voice overrode his morbid thoughts. He pictured her at the cabin, remembered the way she'd teased him or simply sat on the porch step and listened to the sounds of the forest with him. She'd been a good companion.

He groaned with need and crushed her to him, feeling her warmth through the silk. Holding her, in her red dress, was like holding fire in his arms. His taunting had backfired: he was the one being roasted alive.

"So, what do you say?" she demanded, a dare in her eyes. He felt the flaming needles of desire jab deeper.

"About what?" He could hardly think with her breasts pressed to his chest, her thighs nestled against his. He kept seeing winter nights with snow covering the ground, him covering her, keeping her warm....

"Marriage. Shall we give it a try?"

He pulled away so he could look into her eyes. A slight smile pulled at the corner of her gorgeous mouth, but her eyes were like pools reflecting the moonlight, so deep he could drown in their silvery depths.

He realized he was going down for the third time. Time to put an end to this charade. He released her. Tucking her hand into the crook of his elbow, he started toward the house. He managed a strained laugh. "You tempt me, woman, but I'm wise to your ways."

At the door, she tugged her hand free. "Wise, Daniel?" she asked very gently, and left him there, wondering if he was foolishly throwing away something he'd want later... when it was too late.

Chapter Nine

"Daniel came through," Carol announced. "Not a cloud in the sky, not a fly in the ointment." She laughed at her own quip.

Brittney and Harry did, too.

The wedding had gone off without a hitch. The last of the photographs had been snapped. Now they were on their way to the resort for the reception. Beatrice had wanted a formal dinner at the house, but Carol had talked her out of that. A buffet and dance in the ballroom would leave everyone sufficiently tired.

"I'm glad we won't have to clean rice out of the carpets at the house," Carol remarked as the white limousine pulled under the portico and the doorman stepped forward. Beatrice's going-away outfit was waiting for her in a private suite, and the happy couple would leave from there rather than returning to the house.

"Good planning," Harry said, getting out and lending the women a hand. He kept a possessive grip on Carol as they went up the steps. Carol moved adroitly away.

When they entered the ballroom, Daniel was there, directing the staff in placing the flower arrangements that had been sent out from the church in town. He came to them as soon as he finished.

"If I haven't mentioned it, you both look charming," he said, looking them over with his razor-sharp glance.

"Thank you, and in case I haven't mentioned it, you're my favorite uncle," Carol declared. She gave him a kiss on the cheek.

"I'm your only uncle."

Daniel had paid for the entire wedding, including the women's dresses, which had been horribly expensive. Beatrice had been married in a long dress of antique-white linen with hand-tatted lace. Carol and Brittney were lovely in tawny pink linen the color of a peach blushing golden in the sun. They wore wide-brimmed hats and carried tiny parasols filled with flowers as their bouquets. Indeed, he'd been more than generous.

Brittney and Carol laid the parasols on the table where the cake resided in triple-decked splendor. Another table held finger foods; another, champagne and punch.

"Here are our guests," Daniel said.

He and Harry looked marvelous in their formal clothing, one dark, the other blond, both devastatingly handsome. Brittney looked at Harry in sympathy. He was annoying Carol. He wanted to own her, but Carol would never be a man's possession.

Brittney wondered if she was irritating Daniel. Glancing at him, she found his eyes running over her, taking in everything from her old-fashioned upswept hairdo to the linen pumps on her feet. She felt helplessly open to him. He motioned her over.

The four of them formed a reception line. When Hank and Beatrice arrived, the dancing and eating began. Brittney waited to see if Daniel would dance with her. He'd avoided her the past week, although he'd been in and out of the house quite a bit.

She danced with Harry, then Hank. After waltzing with his sister-in-law and niece, Daniel came to her.

"Getting your duty dances out of the way?" she asked, piqued because he looked so grim.

"Keep quiet, Brittney." He sounded tired.

They danced in total silence, the sounds of merriment swirling around them, leaving them in a strange, tense vacuum.

At last he spoke. "You should be pleased. Isn't this what you planned when you got me to invite Hank to the house? You women like to get a man tied up—physically, mentally, emotionally and legally, don't you?"

His attitude chilled any warmth she'd felt in his arms. "Not at all. As an anthropology student, Daniel, you surely know it was men who instituted marriage."

"Ha."

"It's true. When women figured out it was easier to plant grain than go search for it and thus began to acquire *wealth* in the form of land and stored crops, men muscled in and took over. They knew a good thing when they saw it."

He snorted at her view of history.

"Then men realized they couldn't take their land and possessions with them," she went on, "so they needed to make sure they left it to *their* progeny and not some other man's. Thus was marriage born, with its attendant requirement of fidelity—for the female. Men thought it was all right to seduce other men's wives, of course. Bedroom one-upmanship, one might say."

"Since marriage is all to the man's advantage, I'm surprised a liberated woman such as yourself would advocate the institution," he taunted, warming to the battle.

"Well, women are slowly correcting the inequities," she informed him loftily. "And I also know a good thing when I see it." She looked him over as if judging a prize bull at a fair. A flush spread up his neck. She smiled modestly in triumph.

He pulled her closer. "Think you have all the answers, don't you?" he growled in her ear. Then he surprised her by kissing her hand briefly when the dance ended. He walked off and asked the next woman of importance to dance.

Brittney frowned. Sometimes she thought she was getting to Daniel, but at others . . . She sighed.

They cut the cake and poured the champagne. Daniel made a toast that was amusing and touching. Harry made another. The mayor wasn't to be left out. Then Hank gave one of his own. Brittney began to get dizzy on her third glass.

At last Beatrice and Hank left. The guests departed. Brittney heard Carol gently refuse an invitation from Harry to go out after the reception. He looked sulky. Carol came over to her. "Ready to go? I'm beat."

Brittney agreed. Altogether, the wedding and reception had lasted almost six hours. It was going on eleven o'clock.

Daniel drove them home along the tree-shadowed lane. At the house, they said good-night and went to their rooms. For once, Carol didn't barge in to gab until past midnight.

Brittney changed to a long T-shirt and stood at the window. There, on the side lawn, she'd danced with Daniel in the moonlight. There, in the lake, they'd swum and sailed together. On the patio, she'd eaten countless meals with him over the past three years.

A splash in the narrow strip of lake visible to her caught her eye. She watched Daniel's powerful shoulders gleam in the moonlight. An urge to join him prodded her, but she thought better of it.

Closing the curtains, she went to bed and resolutely counted sheep until she fell asleep.

Muggs was putting out steaming dishes when Brittney went into the breakfast room the next morning. He was alone.

"Where's Daniel?" she asked. "Surely he's not sleeping late. He's usually read half the Sunday paper by now." She smiled, determined to be cheerful and not wear her heart on her sleeve.

"There was trouble at the logging mill," Muggs said. He poured her a cup of tea and set it at her place. "He left early this morning."

Disappointment cut into her like a knife. "What happened? Do you know?"

"A problem with a spiked log. The crew boss called just before the wedding—"

"He knew about it yesterday? He didn't say anything." Why hadn't he told her while they were dancing?

"I'm sure he didn't want to spoil the festivities." Muggs picked up the tray. "Mr. Daniel is considerate that way." He walked out with his usual grave dignity.

Brittney sat alone at the table. She was furiously hurt that he hadn't confided in her. Slowly she brought her feelings under control. She didn't own Daniel. He was under no obligation to report his plans to her. She put aside her worries for his safety and considered her future. When Carol came down, Brittney had her course of action planned out.

"I think I'll go home," she announced. "There are no jobs for me up here. In Louisiana, I can work for my grandfather until I find something else."

"Giving up on Daniel?" Carol asked. She didn't seem surprised at Brittney's decision.

"Umm, I think so." Brittney managed a nonchalant shrug.

"You can't leave before my birthday," Carol reminded her. "It's only a week away." She grinned. "I wonder if I can get a trip to Europe out of my dear, hardheaded uncle?"

"Getting away from Harry?"

"He's driving me right up the wall," Carol confessed. "Why do men think they own you just because you date a few times?"

Brittney shrugged again.

"How about a set of tennis? I feel restless."

"Sure." She followed Carol up the stairs to change shoes.

The rest of the week passed in a flurry of activity. Sure enough, Carol got her trip to Europe for her birthday. The tickets arrived in the mail, the tour scheduled only a week away. Brittney gave her friend a travel kit and sightseeing guidebook.

Hank and Beatrice sent a telegram from their cruise ship in Hawaii and a diamond necklace-and-earring set from Tiffany. Harry sent flowers. He'd returned to his job back east. It was time for Brittney to move on, too.

"I'm nearly packed," Carol announced, joining Brittney in the library for a midmorning coffee. Her trip was less than two days away. She was supposed to leave at midnight the next night. "You're probably finished."

Brittney nodded. She was leaving at noon the following day. Carol's idea of being nearly packed was having about three dozen outfits lying about her room. Half of them would have to be left behind. Brittney didn't have that problem. When she left, she would take everything with her—including her bruised but wiser heart.

"I wish you'd come with me," Carol groused. "If you asked nicely, your grandfather would let you."

Brittney shook her head. "I'd rather not."

"Daniel would pay—"

"Absolutely not," Brittney declared.

She was trying very hard not to think of Daniel. He hadn't returned, nor had he called in two weeks.

Carol looked disgruntled, but she understood. "Come help me decide what to wear." The phone rang. Carol picked it up. "Hello?" She listened, her eyes growing wide. "Oh, my God," she said a second later.

Brittney set her cup down. She knew it was bad news by the expression on Carol's face.

"How bad?" Carol asked. "Operating!" Then, "We'll be there as soon as possible." She hung up.

"It's Daniel, isn't it?" Brittney asked, feeling a fatal stab in her heart.

Carol nodded. "He's been hurt. A spiked log, they think."

"How . . . how serious?" Brittney thought of saw blades and splinters flying through the air like shrapnel.

"He was hit in the head—there's a concussion—but the worst is his leg. A piece of spike went through it."

"Dear God," Brittney whispered. "I thought they ran the logs through a metal detector. Why didn't they use a metal detector?" She leaped to her feet. "Where is he?"

"At the local hospital. He's in surgery. We'll fly up, then rent a car." Carol picked up the phone to call a charter company. "We'd better take a few clothes."

They left within the hour, their respective trips forgotten in the face of the emergency. In record time, they arrived at the small town where the logging mill was located. They went directly to the hospital. There they saw the doctor before going to Daniel.

"He's fine," the surgeon assured them. "He won't be getting around quite as fast for several weeks, but he should heal okay. I've pinned the bones together."

"Thank God," Carol murmured.

Her worry showed, more than any words, how much she loved Daniel. Brittney felt closer to her friend than she ever had. When they finished questioning the doctor, they went to Daniel's room. He was asleep, but restless.

"He looks so pale," Brittney whispered, her heart going out to him. He'd hate being an invalid, if only for a few weeks.

For the next three hours, they waited.

"Listen to this," Carol said at one point, looking through the paper she'd brought back from the waiting room. "'After a time of great trial, the Aquarian will come into bliss.'" She looked up at Brittney. "That sounds encouraging, doesn't it?"

Brittney smiled at her friend. Carol looked so distraught, Brittney couldn't ridicule her need to find hope in astrology. "He'll come through with flying colors." She crossed her fingers.

Carol prowled around the small room. "I'll go get us some coffee," she volunteered, and took off after digging change out of her purse.

Brittney sat down in the chair by Daniel's bed. She took his hand in hers and laid it against her cheek for a minute, grateful that he was alive and not injured worse than he was. She was unprepared to hear a raspy but amused voice speak as she planted a row of kisses on his warm skin.

"If this is more of the joy-of-having-a-wife demonstration, I like it."

She gasped and jerked her head up.

Daniel was smiling at her, his face still pale, his eyes tired, but *smiling*. She smiled back, suddenly, gloriously, deliriously happy. He asked for water, then drifted to sleep again. Brittney told Carol the news when she returned. They waited some more. Night came before he woke for a second time.

"How long have you been here?" he asked after glancing around the room and finding them alone.

"Carol and I arrived around noon."

"I thought she was off to Europe." He was hoarse, and she could see it took an effort for him to speak.

"Tomorrow," Brittney said. "We forgot about the trip when we heard you were injured."

"A bean on the head and a broken leg," he scoffed. "I'll be heading for the woods as soon as I'm out of here."

"Not a chance," she told him. "You'll rest until the doctor says you can resume work."

He scowled fiercely. "I'll do as I damned well please."

Her relief lent an edge to her tongue. "Are you insane or just stupid?"

"I've got to protect my men. Someone put a *plastic* spike in that log. I aim to find out who and why."

"That's why the metal detector didn't find it, isn't it?" Brittney asked. She looked at Daniel, lying weak and injured in the hospital bed. "How could anyone be so cruel?"

"Hanging's too good for whoever did it," Daniel declared with narrowed eyes. "First I'll draw and quarter him, then I'll leave him out for bear bait." He pulled his hand from hers and pushed the button for the nurse.

"What is it?" Brittney asked, turning the signal off.

"I want to know how soon I can get out of here."

She sighed. He was going to be one very difficult patient. "The doctor will be by later. You can ask him."

He settled back on his pillow, a sheen of perspiration covering his face. She dampened a washcloth and wiped his face tenderly. He caught her hand and pushed it away.

"Enough of the TLC," he growled. "I'm not helpless yet."

In spite of her exasperation, she was glad to see him in fighting trim. It would take more than a spike to stop her Aquarian man. *Hers? Don't start thinking that way.*

Carol returned with one of the interminable cups of coffee they'd both consumed that day.

"I hope you're not here to nurse me, too," he greeted her. "You women use any excuse to throw your weight around."

"Well, I see your personality wasn't changed by the accident," Carol remarked, tongue in cheek. She set her cup down and leaned over to kiss him on his chin. "But I'm glad you're alive and still kicking like a mule."

"Aren't you supposed to be in Europe?" His tone mellowed somewhat.

Brittney went to the window to give them some privacy. She sipped cold "machine" coffee without noticing its taste.

"Oh, Brittney and I both forgot everything in our rush to get to you," Carol explained. She gestured to their casual slacks and tops. "We came as we were. I suppose we need to call the airlines and cancel our reservations—"

"We?" Daniel asked. "Is Brittney going with you?"

"No, she's going home."

Brittney half turned from the window and looked at him over her shoulder, her glance cool. Their eyes locked.

"Weren't you going to say goodbye?" he asked with a harsh inflection in his voice.

Brittney shrugged. "I didn't know where you were."

"Muggs always knows where I am. You've been around long enough to know that."

"Muggs also knows I'm leaving." She returned his glare steadily. "He could have told you . . . had you asked."

Daniel punched a button that raised his head close to a sitting position. He looked ready for a fight.

"I'll cancel my trip," Carol volunteered hastily. "I'll go with you to check things out at the logging operation."

"No, you won't," Daniel snarled. "That tour cost a bundle. You'll go if I have to throw you on the plane myself. Both of you get on back to the lake house. I'll be there as soon as I can."

"You can't traipse off by yourself. I'm going with you to the cabin," Carol declared.

"No way." Daniel crossed his arms over his chest, wincing as he jostled his throbbing head.

Carol gave Brittney an exasperated glance. Then she snapped her fingers. "Brittney can go with you. She needs a job. You can hire her as your nurse while you recover." When he cast her a fulminating glance, she added, "I won't go to Europe unless she stays with you. Somebody's got to talk sense to you."

"I don't need a nursemaid—" he began.

"I can't—" Brittney started.

"I'll call Mother," Carol interrupted both of them.

His glance should have burned her to a cinder. "All right," he said, turning his gaze to Brittney. "I'll need a secretary. You're hired."

Brittney didn't believe her ears. "You're hiring me as your secretary? What about the one at your office?"

"You'll go with me to the cabin and interface with my staff at the main office," he said decisively. "Now, let me get some sleep. And find out when I can leave this joint." He looked pointedly at Brittney. She nodded. He closed his eyes.

Carol and Brittney tiptoed out.

"Well, you're in," Carol said, letting her breath out with a whoosh. "Make the most of it." She shook her head. "He's going to be a terrible boss."

"I know." Brittney wasn't at all sure she should stay, but she didn't want to cause Carol to miss the grand tour. She resigned herself to fate. "Have a good trip. Don't worry about Daniel."

"I won't." Carol hesitated. "Don't let him hurt you. Men can be cruel when they're running scared."

Brittney chewed on her lip. "Do you think he is?"

"Yeah."

Ten days later, when they arrived at the cabin, Brittney wasn't sure. Daniel had been polite or peevish by turns. Right now he was cursing while a big lumberjack picked him up and carried him inside as if he were a baby.

"Dammit, Clyde, put me down. I can walk. Get my crutches, Brittney," he ordered—futilely, as it turned out. Clyde, one of the largest men she'd ever seen, ignored his boss and packed him inside where the bed was already turned back. Clyde put Daniel down as gently as a babe. Then he stood back and grinned.

"Okay, get back to work. We've all admired your muscles," Daniel snapped.

Sam appeared in the doorway to the kitchen. "Hey, boss, you hungry? I've got stew ready."

"Why aren't you up at camp?"

"The men already ate. Dinah's helping Sam Li with the dishes."

"Daniel has had lunch," Brittney put in. "He needs a nap now. That was thoughtful of you to prepare something, Sam. We'll have it for dinner, if you don't mind."

Sam gave her a big grin. "Glad to see you here. He needs somebody who can handle him."

Brittney ignored the snort from the bed. She laid down her purse and covered Daniel with a sheet.

He flung it off. "Clyde, take me up to the camp—"

"He'll do no such thing. You need to rest." Brittney turned to the other two men. "I'll call you if I need you."

They quickly left, hiding smiles behind hands or mustaches.

"Think you're in charge, huh?" Daniel demanded. "Just because the surgeon said—"

He stopped as Brittney leaned over him, her mouth dangerously close to his as she smoothed the cover. "Daniel," she said, "would you please shut up?" She straightened. "You're to have a nap every afternoon."

A slow smile spread over his face. "Only if you'll give me a kiss to help me sleep."

Her pulse leaped at the visions his statement produced. She'd thought often of kissing him good-night...when they shared the same bed. Playing his game, she bent forward once more.

Anticipation rioted through her as she moved temptingly just within reach. "If I do, you'll quit arguing and do as I tell you?"

"Maybe."

"Your word, Daniel." She hovered an inch from his mouth.

He frowned at her, then his hand came up and caught her behind the neck. He brought her lips to his.

The contact was delicious. Sweet, heady, hot, a thousand other things she couldn't describe. It was the first time he'd touched her, really touched her, since the wedding.

He caressed her with his lips. He played games with her, his tongue stroking and tasting before demanding admittance. When she opened her mouth, he invaded, laving her senses with pure pleasure.

With a tug of his hand, he caused her to lose her balance. She found herself lying across his chest. "I'll hurt you," she said worriedly, trying to ease her weight off him.

"No," he told her. His arm closed around her, holding her captive. "This doesn't hurt nearly as much as wanting you and not being able to touch."

"I never said you couldn't touch me."

"I know," he growled, nibbling at her ear through the tangle of her curls. "That only made it worse."

"Oh."

She turned her face, wanting his kiss again. He didn't deny either of them. They shared the pent-up hunger that had built during the past ten days. Brittney thought she would faint from bliss. He felt good and solid and wonderful.

"God, you taste like honey," he murmured, pausing for breath. He tucked her head against his neck. "Stay with me."

"I . . . I can't."

"Why not? Take a nap with me. You need it as much as I do. You stayed at the hospital until all hours. You drove up here over that winding road all morning. Sleep, Brittney. Nothing else." He chuckled in resignation. "A beautiful woman in my bed, and I can't do a damned thing about it."

"Daniel—"

"Stay," he whispered.

"Let me take my shoes off."

"Promise you'll come back?" He nuzzled along her temple. His hand strayed tantalizingly near her breast.

"I promise."

She kicked her sandals aside. "Do you want your robe off?" She'd brought pajamas and a robe for him. To get him into pants, she'd have had to cut one side open.

"Yeah."

She helped him get it off, treating him as much more of an invalid than he was. She knew she was spoiling him by letting him get his own way so much. He'd soon be impossible to live with.

"Here," he said, moving over and giving her room. She lay down beside him, careful of his injured leg.

"I'm not made of glass," he said, pulling her close. He began rubbing her back in big, slow circles. Her eyes drifted closed. The last thing she felt was his lips against her brow.

When she woke, she was alone. Daniel's voice from the kitchen led her in that direction. He was on the phone, giving orders to his foreman, she surmised.

He had dressed himself in a blue long-sleeved shirt and a pair of faded black cords, split along one seam. He wore thick socks on both feet, covering the cast so that his hurt foot appeared of grotesque proportions.

"I'll be up in the morning," he said, and hung up.

She was alarmed. "You're not going anywhere. The doctor said if you were to fall or injure—"

"Don't tell me what to do," he growled, pivoting on the cast. "I'm a grown man. You're my secretary, not my mother."

She swallowed her worry over his leg and the quick hurt at his curt words. "You're right. I apologize."

She left the room and went out the front door. She walked to the end of the porch and leaned her weight against her hands on the railing. She'd overstepped the bounds. It was one of the things a man like Daniel would hate in a woman...and never permit. She blinked a film of moisture from her eyes.

The thud of his footsteps as he walked with the crutches sounded on the pine floor. She heard him come outside and let the screen door slam behind him. He came to where she stood.

"I'm sorry," he said.

She shook her head without looking at him. "No, you had every right to be angry. I understand completely."

"Do you?" His voice was low, husky, very near.

"My mother and grandfather were always deciding my life for me. I...didn't like it. I was wrong to interfere in yours."

He didn't say anything. After a minute, she heard him sigh. She became aware of sounds around them—the far-off drone of a saw, a truck motor in the distance, birds in the fir trees around them. A patch of sunlight flickered restlessly on the grass near the cabin as the breeze stirred the leaves. Her own soul was restless, too. Perhaps she'd made a mistake in coming here.

"How about some tea or lemonade?" he asked, easing away from her. He sat in a wooden chair and stretched his leg in front of him, the lines of his face weary.

She went inside and found frozen lemonade. She scouted out a pitcher and made the drink. She brought two glasses and a plate of cookies to the porch. After placing his on a tiny table at his elbow, she sat on the top step and took a sip of lemonade.

"Tell me about your childhood," he requested.

It was the first time he'd ever asked about her past, other than casual conversation, usually with Carol present. "It was like any other, I suppose. I went to school. I took piano and ballet." She turned so she could see him, her back against a post.

"What did you like best? What subjects were you good at? Who was your boyfriend?" His mouth lifted in a playful smile at this last question.

Brittney gazed into the distance. "I liked school okay. Ballet was fun, piano a chore. I went to private school in town and was driven back and forth by the chauffeur every day. Mostly I played by myself after school and in summer."

His expression became thoughtful. "That sounds lonely for a young girl. You're a sociable person."

"No, I loved it. I roamed all over the plantation, either on foot or on an old pony the gardener let me use." She remembered sunny days that lasted forever, and heat, and June bugs buzzing about. "I inspected the crops and the river—"

"The Mississippi?"

"No, the Red River. Did you know nearly every Southern state has a Red River? Louisiana, Texas, Tennessee..." She stopped talking, apparently engrossed in her inner thoughts.

Daniel thought of all the things he knew about her; important things such as her loyalty, honesty, humor, pride. But he'd never discovered the details of her life, the little things that had made her happy or sad.

"Did you have a dog?" he asked.

She shook her head. "My mother and grandfather agreed on that. Neither liked pets very much."

And both agreed that she should marry and produce an heir. He thought of the man on the phone who'd asked her to marry him. Her grandfather's choice. Her mother preferred the governor's son or somebody like that. His anger returned, not with Brittney but with her family. They had no right to make such demands. He realized her life probably hadn't been any easier than his.

"What was your favorite food?" he asked.

"I loved turnip greens, all slathered with vinegar so that I could hardly breathe when I ate them. And corn bread like

Tilda, the gardener's wife, made. She let me eat with them sometimes at lunch—she called it 'dinner'—but I had to have dinner, which she called 'supper,' at the main house.''

Slowly a picture of her youth emerged. He sensed from what she didn't say that she'd been alone a lot, but not lonely. She was a person who could entertain herself.

She'd loved shiny rocks. ''I used to collect them along the riverbank. I'd search for hours as if I expected to find gold.'' She laughed.

He thought of his own youth. His parents had been middle-aged, but Adam had been an indulgent older brother. Adam had taken Daniel and his friends on camping trips every summer. Adam had been the one who'd cheered for him in Little League and let him tag along to movies when he had a date. A great older brother.

Daniel suddenly wondered if he'd resented Beatrice's taking all of Adam's time when they fell in love and married. He frowned, his gaze going to Brittney. It was natural for a man to want to be with a woman when he was attracted. He ought to know. He had fought his desire to dash down to the lake house and see Brittney every time she visited for years. He'd always lost.

Careful, he warned. If a man gave an inch, the woman would take over. Women wanted to order a man about like a kid, the way Brittney had earlier, telling him what he could or couldn't do. He wouldn't be led around by the nose like some prize bull by any woman, no matter how attractive he found her.

''Is this leading to a confidence that you still like pretty rocks?'' he asked with a sardonic grin. He gestured at the birthstone ring on her hand.

''I've never had much jewelry, although my grandmother's stuff will come to me someday, I think. I like sapphires best—''

"Come off it. You know I meant diamonds." When she looked blank, he added, "As in rings, engagement and such."

He saw a flicker of hurt in her eyes again, just as he had earlier when he'd spoken sharply. He refused to apologize again. Blast women, anyway. They had only to look morose and a man groveled to make them happy again.

She recovered quickly. "Why, Daniel, are you offering?" she asked with a pretty flutter of lashes, wringing a laugh out of him.

"Not on your life. A ring is a noose, to my way of thinking."

"But then," she offered sweetly, "your thinking has been rather muddled lately, hasn't it?" Before he could think of a retort, she jumped up. "I'm going for a walk. Would you like me to drive you up to the camp in the morning, boss?"

She smiled brightly, waiting for his answer. He wanted to demand that she stay with him, that she not go off alone. He clenched his jaw. "Yes," he said.

He watched her skip down the steps and head across the yard. She raised her arms over her head and clasped her hands, stretching out the kinks along her spine. He felt the stir of desire beat through his blood.

He'd given up most of his freedom and all of his personal dreams a long time ago. When Brittney was around, he got insane ideas about recapturing them. As if he had time. Archaeology was a pursuit long past for him.

He breathed the fresh, clean scent of the forest. It occurred to him that there were other dreams, such as living up here.... Forget it. He had too many responsibilities to hibernate in the woods.

As for Brittney, he would not fall for the tender trap of her arms. But it was hard not to, he admitted. And getting harder each day.

Chapter Ten

Brittney was exasperated. Being with Daniel day after day was wonderful, except she wanted more. He treated her with indulgent humor—a cross between an efficient employee and a favored niece. If she'd thought they'd draw closer due to his injury, she could forget it. He was more distant than ever.

He wasn't her only problem. Her grandfather wanted her to come home—now. He had threatened to disinherit her. Her mother was worried and had called several times. Often, Brittney wanted to confide in Daniel, but she couldn't dump her woes on him.

She waited for him now, sitting in the truck, a book propped open on the steering wheel. Daniel stood in a small clearing, talking to one of the section foremen. The crews were making careful visual inspections of the trees. They'd found another plastic spike.

A shout drew her attention. Paul came out of the trees, his big Belgians straining hauling a huge log. He waved to her when he had a chance. She loved watching him and the horses. They worked together as a skillful team, bringing logs to the road so more trails wouldn't have to be cut into the forest. The Montclair company did only thin-cutting, never clear-cutting, which involved chopping down everything in sight and left the land and wildlife exposed to the elements.

"Hey, dreamboat, how's it going?" Paul came over to the truck and leaned his arms on the open window. He had his shirt off, and his chest was bronze, his brown hair gold-streaked from the sun. He was a fine specimen of a man.

"Okay. How about yourself?" Brittney closed the book.

"Can't complain. You've been here ten days now. Time you had a break. There's a dance in town tomorrow night. Want to go?"

Brittney automatically glanced toward Daniel. He was listening to his foreman, but his eyes were on her and Paul. She almost expected him to shake his head at her, as if he could hear what Paul and she were discussing.

"Won't the dragon let you out of his lair?" Paul teased.

"Daniel isn't my keeper," she said, annoyed with herself for letting him influence her life. First her mother, then her grandfather, and now Daniel. It was time she stood on her own two feet. She smiled into Paul's handsome face. "I'd love to go. How dressy is it?"

"Oh, something you'd go out to dinner in. Say, how about dinner first? We could go into town early, about six, eat, then go over to the dance. How's that sound?"

"I like it," she said, laughing at the way he planned things right on the spot. She liked his laid-back manner. Her being out of the cabin would give Daniel some breathing space, too, since he valued his solitude so much.

During their ten days in the mountains, she'd tried to stay out of his way when not following orders. Usually she spent

MAN FROM THE NORTH COUNTRY 161

the morning typing letters he'd written in his neat script and talking to his secretary in Minneapolis, gathering information he wanted and relaying orders through her. In the afternoons, she drove him around the various sites. They usually had lunch and dinner at the camp kitchen. After dinner, she read and Daniel consulted with Paul and Dinah about the planting-and-cutting schemes. There was more work to running the operation than she'd realized.

"See ya' at six tomorrow." Paul pushed himself off the truck and went back to work. "Wear something soft and pretty." He winked, then waved as he picked up the reins.

Daniel was frowning when he came over to the truck, but she didn't notice. She'd had an idea. She waited until he'd handed her the crutches and slowly hefted himself inside, having made it clear to her and the men that he wanted no help.

"Daniel, do you think it'd work if you used a dog to sniff out the plastic spikes? In this book I'm reading, the hero uses a dog to track the criminals through the woods. Maybe whoever is putting in the spikes leaves a scent. If you used the one you found—"

"Clyde, come here for a minute, will you?" he yelled, cutting off the rest of her words.

The huge lumberjack hustled over.

"Do you still have that bird dog you used to brag about?"

"Yeah, boss." Clyde looked questioningly at Daniel.

"Think he could sniff out spikes?"

A gleam came into the man's eyes. "Damn, uh, darn right, he could. Just give him a chance."

"All right. He's on the payroll. How soon can you get him up here?"

"An hour if I call my wife to bring him."

Daniel handed him the truck phone. In a few minutes, the matter was taken care of. Clyde went back to work.

"Let's go to H-37," Daniel said, naming a section and sector of the forest to be cut next.

Brittney started the truck and eased off the brake. She drove like an expert on the rough roads now. Daniel had coached her.

"That was a good idea," he said.

"Thanks, but it was the book and Paul's horses that made me think of it."

They were silent for a mile. Brittney was aware of Daniel's gaze on her in a relentless study. She began to feel uneasy. She had displeased him, she could tell. "What is it?" she finally asked, unable to bear the suspense a second longer.

"Why did Paul tell you to wear something soft and pretty?"

The harsh question startled her. "I didn't realize you'd heard us," she said. She felt defensive, even though she'd done nothing wrong.

"Answer the question," he ordered.

He was back to being the autocratic male. It made her furious, but she wouldn't let him see that. "Why?" she asked pertly. "Would you like me to wear something soft and pretty for you?"

"You're not going out with him," Daniel stated.

"Yes, I am."

"Brittney—"

"I'm an adult, and you're not my daddy, Daniel," she reminded him softly, using words similar to those he'd used when he'd told her he was a man who wasn't going to take orders from her. It worked both ways.

"He's broken more hearts than a dog has fleas," he informed her in a tone that questioned her good sense.

"He won't break mine." She gave Daniel a teasing glance from under her lashes and added, "You already did that."

There, that should give him something to think about. She felt somewhat mean for baiting him, but decided he deserved it. "Don't worry about me. I'm a big girl now, and I can handle men."

"The way you handled me?" he suggested, reminding her of dances in the moonlight, of kisses shared under the stars.

A flush crept up her neck and into her face. "Perhaps."

His hand closed into a fist and came down on the cast covering his thigh. "Dammit, I'm telling you for your own good—"

"Don't come on as the concerned uncle, Daniel. It won't wash. Why don't you just admit you can't stand other men around me?"

Harsh silence greeted this cool assessment. She kept a smile on her face with an effort. Daniel was now the one who was furious. She didn't care. She was tired of guarding her emotions around him, of being careful not to offend or bother or smother or whatever it was he thought women did to him.

"All right. I can't stand other men around you." He crossed his arms over his chest.

The admission stunned her. What should she do? She slowed the truck for a steep grade. Risking a quick glance at him, she detected triumph in the smile lurking around his hard mouth.

The devil! He was trying to manipulate her. "I'm still going to the dance with Paul tomorrow night."

"Over my dead body."

"That can be arranged." She didn't dare look his way after that. He probably had smoke coming out of his ears.

After a minute, he began speaking in a reasonable tone. "You don't understand, kitten. Sometimes these dances can get rough. The men are full of high spirits after a month in the woods. They drink a little and then, well, usually a fight breaks out between the cowboys and the loggers.''

She hated him calling her by a pet name when it meant nothing. ''I'm sure Paul and our men can watch out for me.''

Daniel suddenly wanted to do damage to something. Brittney, for all her accommodating ways, could be damned stubborn. If she wanted to get involved with a Don Juan like Paul, who was he to stop her?

But he missed her pursuit of him, he finally admitted to himself. During the past ten days, she'd been the perfect employee—always cheerful no matter how cantankerous he was, prompt to follow his directions and correct in her manner toward him. She no longer flirted outrageously, or endlessly reminded him of the advantages of marriage. She didn't have to. He knew them all by heart.

Night after night he'd lain alone in his narrow bed, thinking of those three hundred sixty-five nights she'd mentioned. During the evening, when she went to her room and read her book, he'd wanted to demand that she return and talk to him. Some nights he'd made up reasons for her to stay, or given her extra work. She did the chores, then left.

Had she given up on him? Apparently. Well, it was what he wanted, wasn't it? He had no time to devote to courtship and love and all that stuff. Whatever dreams he'd had along those lines had dried up long ago. But it had been fun. They'd been playing games with the man-woman thing, and it had added an edge to life.

He rubbed his aching leg and wished the cast was off. He couldn't dance in the moonlight now. But there were other things he could do—like hold her and kiss her and caress her. He groaned as needs better ignored roared to blazing life.

"Does your leg hurt?" she asked, breaking into his tumultuous thoughts.

There was concern in her eyes. He could appeal to her sympathy and ask her to stay.... No, he couldn't. "No. I'm fine." He closed his eyes and wished it were true.

Brittney put on a sleeveless cotton dress that showed off her smooth shoulders. The material was blue, a color universally liked by men. The full skirt swirled around her knees in a sensuous fashion, its hem scalloped to show the white prairie-style petticoat with a lacy ruffle around the bottom.

After putting on her high-heeled sandals, she picked up a warm shawl and a beaded purse and went out on the porch. Daniel was reading a report. He barely glanced up.

Paul arrived on time. He drove a red convertible with a white top. The two-seater sports car looked fast and wicked.

"I love your car," she exclaimed when he got out and came across the lawn. She took a second to admire his bronzed good looks, too. He wore dress boots, dark slacks and a sport jacket in shades of blue with brown and beige. His light beige shirt contrasted nicely with a blue and brown tie. He looked as dashing as a movie hero.

"Umm," he said. "Soft and *gorgeous*."

"Thank you."

Daniel gave a snort behind his report.

"Evening, boss," Paul said. He grinned at Brittney.

Daniel put down the papers. He looked the pair over before returning the greeting. Brittney thought he was going to tell them not to stay out late, but he merely chatted with Paul about the weather for a couple of minutes.

"Ready?" Paul asked. Taking her arm, he guided her to the flashy car and tucked her inside.

She waved to Daniel as they drove off. He waved back without smiling.

They ate at a wonderful Italian restaurant down the street from the hospital where Daniel had been. The dance was at a saloon-type building a few blocks from there. All the single loggers were there, mostly dressed in jeans that looked new, with white shirts and fancy boots. The cowboys were outfitted the same. So were a lot of the women.

"It's a friendly crowd," Paul assured her.

They joined the gang.

"Does the boss know she's out with you?" one of the bolder of the men asked Paul.

Paul grinned. "He was sitting right on the porch. I drove up, whisked her into the car and left before he cleared leather."

Brittney joined in the laughter. A picture of Daniel drawing a six-shooter lingered in her mind. He'd have made a great sheriff in the old West—steady, steely-eyed and incorruptible.

Taking a deep breath, she banished him from her mind. Tonight belonged to her, darn it. And she was going to have fun.

A five-piece band assembled their instruments, tuned up and swung into a Texas two-step. She was amazed at the mass surge to the floor. Everyone had the urge to dance, it seemed.

The music swept them around in a big circle. Brittney felt as if she were on a merry-go-round. She was introduced to the other women as she and Paul danced past the couples. At two o'clock, when the dance was over, she realized she had had a good time.

After shouts of farewell, Paul put her in his car and they started back to the cabin. When the road became a gravel lane, he stopped and pushed a button. The top lowered. He resumed the drive, going very slow. The moonlight was heavenly.

"Too cool?" he asked, solicitous of her.

"No. It's wonderful." She rested her head on the seat and gazed up at the stars. Once she'd teased Daniel about taking a moonlight ride in a flashy red convertible, she remembered. That had been a little over two months ago, but it seemed a year. She'd thought to taunt Daniel then, make him notice her as a woman.

She'd succeeded, but she'd also fallen deeply, truly in love with him. She'd outwitted only herself. She smiled at her foolish idea of bringing Daniel to his knees. She was the one brought low.

Her heart seemed heavy in her chest. No doubt it was filled with the irony of life, she mocked herself.

Paul pulled into the clearing and stopped. He turned to her. "Are you in love with Daniel, Brittney?" he asked gently.

"Yes."

He smiled and leaned over her. His kiss made no demand. It was brief; a farewell from one friend to another. "I hope you enjoyed tonight. Sometimes it helps to get away in order to see things more clearly."

"I had a lovely time, Paul. Thank you." She stroked his lean cheek, grateful for his friendship.

He escorted her to the porch. She stood there and watched him drive away. Paul would be safe to date, she thought. He hadn't expected too much. The thought made her sad. Paul knew she had nothing to give him. She sat on the porch, her feet on the step below, and rested her elbows on her knees.

"That was touching," a voice said behind her.

Startled, Brittney jumped, and whirled around. Daniel was standing just inside the door, almost invisible behind the screen. He opened it and came outside. He wasn't using his crutches, she noted, but walked by swinging his cast out and ahead of him.

"Was it?" She smiled. "We had a good time. The men didn't fight. We danced the two-step all night, around and around."

An ominous silence greeted her recital. Daniel was making her nervous—deliberately, she thought. He continued standing just behind and to the side of her. She turned slightly so she could look up at him.

"Was tonight a ploy to make me jealous?" he inquired.

"Did it?" she asked with a catchy laugh, as if they were still playing the courting game as they had at Lake Minnetonka.

Except somehow the rules had been changed, and she didn't have the new set. She was no longer sure what her position was. They were on Daniel's turf now. They played by his rules.

"You know how to push all the buttons, don't you?"

She realized he was furious with her. "Think what you like," she told him, suddenly tired of it all. "Or whatever your ego demands." She rose, brushed past him and went to the door. "As soon as you get your cast off, I'll be heading for Louisiana," she informed him. She swept inside and into her room.

He followed and flung the door open. She gasped, not in fear, but in fury. He thumped across the floor, his cast making sounds like thunder.

"Tell me the wonders of marriage," he invited in a snarl. "Tell me how great the man-woman relationship can be. Tell me about love and fidelity and all that stuff you toss around like confetti. I want to hear some more."

She stared at him.

"No? Then we'll just have to demonstrate, won't we?"

He enfolded her in his arms—not harshly as she expected, but tenderly. She could have fought harshness, but she had no defense against gentleness. His lips caressed hers until she opened her mouth to his. The kiss lasted a long time. When they were both weak with longing, he released her mouth.

"Tell me how much you want me, Brittney. Describe the joys of marriage like you did before...the touching and making love, the sharing, the companionship and being there for each other. Make me see it," he coaxed, his voice rough with needs she couldn't begin to decipher. "Make me forget the doubts I have when I'm away from you. Make me want this marriage the way I want you every time I see you."

His eyes blazed over her, and for a minute she witnessed the passion she'd wanted to find. It wasn't enough. Daniel had been right. She wanted him: heart, soul, body; all the ways there were.

She shook her head. "I can't. You'll have to discover it for yourself. I was wrong to think I could talk you into..." She didn't say love, but the word trembled on her tongue.

They stood there beside her bed. A minute ticked past, then another. Tension gathered inside her. She knew he wouldn't hurt her, but he was frustrated and angry. And he was still Daniel, her first love, and he could seduce her with only a touch.

At last he let her go, his eyes dark as night, as haunted as an empty mansion. Without a word, he left.

When his steps ceased behind the closed door of his own room, Brittney sank onto the bed, trying to figure out just what had happened between them. Something had, but what?

If she hadn't known better, she'd have thought she had broken through the icy shell he maintained and pierced right to his heart.

No. All she'd ever reached in Daniel was the fiery passion he possessed. How could she have been so foolish to think it was the same as love?

Chapter Eleven

Brittney leaned her elbows on the table in the dining tent and read the five postcards that had arrived that day. Carol was having a wonderful time. She'd met some very nice people on the tour. Greece was her favorite country, so far. And she had decided she wanted to learn the family business when she returned home. Would Brittney please suggest the idea to Daniel and see what kind of reaction she got?

Brittney glanced at Daniel. He was in conference with Paul and Dinah. They had rolls of papers that looked like blueprints, but were topography maps of the various sectors. A fire was burning in the state forest, and they were planning firebreaks in case it reached this area.

Clyde came in. He left Hilda, his dog, outside. He swore the dog would climb trees to get a bird. Brittney liked listening to his tales of the north woods.

"How's Hilda doing?" she asked when he sat at her table to rest and drink a cup of strong coffee. He ate two pastries in about four bites.

"She's a good dog. Found two spikes in the new section we started yesterday. We're heading out there to finish it this morning." Clyde shook his head. "Can't figure out who's the culprit. We haven't seen any of those nature radicals around. We tried following a trail, but the bast—uh, person is smart. Headed right for the creek."

"He knows the woods," she mused. "Could it be someone who's working here, one of the crew, a mole like in the spy books?"

He shook his big, shaggy head. "I know 'em all. We haven't had anyone new since the spring hiring."

It was a worrying puzzle.

"Well, I've got to get back to work."

"Take it easy," she said, smiling. He waved over his shoulder to her. She liked the men who worked here. They were good at their jobs and knew it. Their casual arrogance, coupled with a cheerful disposition, was appealing. Daniel was the same way when he relaxed. At the present, though, he wasn't. He was much too concerned about the mysterious spiker to relax.

One more week, she counted, and the cast could come off. Then she'd leave. She had called her family and told them to expect her home for Labor Day.

"A penny for them," Paul said.

The conference was evidently over. Dinah gave her a smile and left the tent. Daniel was still scowling at the charts. He had become the ice man again, remote as a granite peak.

"I was thinking of my family. My grandfather gives a gigantic party over the holiday, complete with overnight guests and a ball."

"Shades of Tara," Paul teased, a hand over his heart.

"Exactly," Brittney agreed. "Even the governor at-
nds. My grandfather is one of his biggest supporters."

"And the governor's son?" Daniel asked in a hard voice.

Brittney faced him. "Yes. He'll be sliding down the ban-
ters and swinging from the chandeliers—"

"How old is he?" Daniel asked, puzzled.

"Ten, and a holy terror. My mother detests him."

Daniel studied her through narrowed eyes. "I thought she
anted you to marry him."

"Oh, that's the governor's cousin. He works with my
rother at the oil refinery." She remembered Carol's letter
nd had an idea. "Carol wants a job when she comes home
ext month. You know, Daniel, if you trained her to take
ver the printing company and my brother to take over the
apermaking operation, you could spend most of your time
p here. Did you ever think of that?"

She was excited by this plan. It would get Sonny away
om her grandfather, who paid him too little for the work
e did, and away from his rich friends, who caused him to
end more than he had. It would give Carol a chance to use
er business degree, and it would free Daniel to live the life
e enjoyed. Perfect.

"No," Daniel replied. "What job do you want?"

Brittney studied him. He was tough, hard and cynical, but
e could be gentle, so very gentle. "My grandfather has one
ll picked out for me," she told him.

His face darkened. He picked up the crutches and headed
ut. "There's work to be done," he said harshly. "Let's
ead for the new sector. Clyde's going over it again with the
og."

She followed him to the truck. She'd made him angry
gain, but she wasn't sure why. She mentally shook her
ead, giving up. Daniel was too unpredictable these days.

Paul mounted one of his horses and rode into the tree
following a narrow trail. He'd beat them to the job site. Sh
started down the road as soon as Daniel was settled. H
black mood permeated the cab of the vehicle. That wa
nothing new; he'd been in a foul mood all week.

They arrived at the site to find bedlam had broken loose
"We caught him. He's heading down the back trail," Clyd
yelled at them. "The spiker. He's on a dirt bike."

Paul was already there as expected. He thundered pas
them. "Head him off at the crossroad. I'll chase him dow
that way." He was gone, the horse's hooves throwing up
blizzard of dirt.

Brittney threw the truck into reverse, turned, then heade
back down the road at a furious pace. She was determine
not to let the saboteur escape.

"Stop!" Daniel ordered, grabbing her arm.

"You heard what Paul said. We can head him off at—'

"Not you!" he roared. "Clyde can do it. Get back u
there. He'll drive."

"We haven't time," she gasped, wrenching the whee
around a narrow turn, a steep drop-off less than a foot fror
the front tire. "We might lose him."

"Dammit, Brittney. Stop this truck! You'll break you
fool neck."

She spared a grin at that. "Afraid for yours, Daniel? I ca
let you out."

He subsided, grumbling under his breath about hard
headed women. Poor Daniel. With his sense of protective
ness toward females, she was trying his patience to the limit
And the chase had hardly begun.

She put the gas pedal to the floorboard on a straigh
stretch. When they reached the fork in the road, she brake
and cut the engine. In the silence, they could hear the nois
of a dirt bike.

"Good, we made it," Brittney said in satisfaction. The woods on either side of the road were too dense for him to cut through them around the truck. Above them, she heard Paul give a shout. He was enjoying himself.

Daniel climbed out of the truck. So did she. They waited for the man on the bike to come into view. What if he couldn't stop in time and ran over Daniel? What if he had a gun? She picked up a thick stick. Daniel gave her an exasperated look.

"Stay out of it," he warned.

The man—young, about twenty-two or -three, she guessed—slid to a halt when he realized he was trapped. Although Paul was still out of sight on the trail, they could hear him coming their way.

The biker weighed his chances and decided he'd come out better against a woman and a cripple. He tossed the small bike aside and came straight at Daniel, his fists ready.

Daniel ducked and landed a glancing blow on the young man's chin, but not being able to move, he caught the next hook on his jaw and a jab into his midsection that took his breath.

Brittney couldn't just stand there. She hit the guy on the head with her weapon. The stick broke without even fazing him. Before he could turn on her, she flung herself on his back and wrapped her arms around him. The three of them went down in a flurry of dust and leaves.

Brittney lost her grip and ended on the bottom of the pile while Daniel grappled with the miscreant. Before she was mashed into pulp, Paul arrived. He jumped into the fray and in less than a minute, the man was subdued. Paul hauled him to his feet, with his arms twisted behind his back.

"Get the lead rope off the rein," he ordered.

Brittney did. In a moment, the young man was securely tied. Daniel, cursing worse than any sailor she'd ever heard, struggled to his feet. She brushed dirt off him and looke anxiously at his cast. It was cracked along the top.

"Oh, Daniel, your leg," she cried.

"It's okay," he snapped at her. He called the sheriff o the car phone while Paul guarded the prisoner. "There's deputy on the main road. He'll be here in fifteen minutes," he reported.

"I recognize this guy," Paul said.

"Yeah," Daniel agreed, looking the man over. "Bi Limmer. Clyde hired him as a topper back in the spring. W had to get rid of him. He was a sloppy worker, dangerous t the crew."

"I was faster than anybody you had." Limmer spat in th dust near Daniel's foot.

Brittney started toward him, still furious that he'd a tacked Daniel. Daniel caught her arm in an unbreakabl grip.

She mastered her instinctive need to slap the young man' sneering face. They waited for the policeman. The wood around them were eerily quiet. She knew the animal wouldn't stir again until the human intruders were gone.

After the deputy arrived, they returned to the logging site Clyde explained that Hilda had sniffed the guy out an they'd come upon him red-handed, driving one of the spike into a tree. He'd had several more with him. Paul explaine the chase, Daniel the fight. Brittney waited quietly in th truck. Her hands were trembling with aftershock.

When it was over and the deputy drove off, the forme logger handcuffed in the back of his patrol car, Daniel piv oted and looked at her. He didn't say anything for a lon minute. Brittney stared at him, somehow knowing what h was going to say before the words left his mouth.

"Clyde," he ordered, "take Brittney to the cabin to pac her things, then get her down to the airport and have Joe fl her to Minneapolis. I'll call to let him know you're on the way." He turned around and began handing out orders to the crew.

Brittney fought the rising tears until they were out of sight of the sector camp. Clyde handed her a handkerchief. She cried silently into it. When they reached the cabin, she quickly packed, careful to leave nothing behind.

Paul was talking to his horse, rubbing down the sweating hide of the Belgian after their run.

"Thing is," he said, "if I had a little filly that thought as much of me as that one does of you, I'd be treating her with kid gloves. Gentle-like, you know. Not sending her off just because she tried to help out in a fight. Did a good job, too."

Daniel, sitting in a sling chair with his leg propped on a stump, ignored his friend. His scowl was as dark as the woods on a moonless night. He was still furious with her for throwing herself into danger. He still wanted to either shake her or make love to her. If they had gone back to the cabin, he knew which it would have been. He'd had to send her away. For her own good.

"Yessir," Paul continued, lifting a hoof as wide as his hand could span and cleaning the dirt out of the frog, "I'd treat her right. Like a queen. If I had a woman sweet on me—"

"You can knock it off," Daniel snarled, starting up from the chair and pacing the clearing. He ran a hand through his hair.

"We could catch her if we hurried," Paul remarked, dropping the hoof. "I could take you down in the Jeep. You probably need to go to town anyway. The doc should check that leg."

"I'd make a lousy husband," Daniel said to no one in particular. "I'd hurt her."

"She's pretty tough, for a sweet young thing."

Daniel clenched and unclenched one hand. "She probably hates me. I tried to drive her away. I didn't want entanglements."

"And now?"

He didn't want to admit it. It left him open, vulnerable. It would change his life.

What was so wonderful about his present mode of living?

Nothing, he realized. He still had all the responsibilities of life, but none of the rewards. Like a fool, he'd denied himself the sweetest reward of all—Brittney and the joy he'd find in her. She'd tried to convince him of the advantages of marriage, but he'd been too stupid to see that he needed only her. She was the real advantage. She'd give him all her love, her loyalty. She'd defend him to the death. A man would be a fool to give all that up.

"Well?" Paul demanded.

"I love her," Daniel replied.

Paul grinned, threw the crutches into the Jeep and held the door open. "What are we waiting for?"

Clyde looked as miserable as Brittney felt as they bumped along the county road on the way to town. The weather was hot, but summer was over for her. The chill of autumn had settled into her soul. Why had she ever started her crazy pursuit of Daniel?

She sighed, still shaken by the fight and the sudden dismissal. Tears misted her eyes. She blinked them away angrily. She was not going to cry over Daniel Montclair.

Let him live his life in solitude. The Aquarius man, rugged, self-sufficient, independent—he needed nothing and no one. She knew that now. Never again would she make such a fool of herself.

"There's somebody behind us," Clyde said, peering into the rearview mirror.

Three blasts from a horn caused her to swivel around to see what was going on. "It's Paul," she said. "And Daniel."

Her heart gave a gigantic leap and began pounding.

"They want us to stop, I think." Clyde pulled over to the side of the road.

She wanted to take off and outrun them to the small airstrip west of town, but that would be silly. Daniel probably remembered something else he needed Clyde to do in town. Or maybe he was going to see about his ruined cast. She steeled herself to face him. She'd do it with a smile, she vowed.

Daniel looked grim when he climbed out of the Jeep. He came to the truck. "Paul will take you back," he said to Clyde. "Brittney can take me to the doctor."

Before she could even consider a refusal, Daniel had climbed into the truck, forcing her behind the wheel.

"What's going on?" she asked. Her hands trembled. She gripped the steering wheel.

"Would you take me to the doctor?" he asked in a surprisingly gentle tone.

Behind them, Paul made a U-turn and left as soon as Clyde was inside. There was no one else to drive him.

"Am I reinstated?" she quipped. Her laughter was shaky, too.

"Yes," he said. He sighed and was quiet.

She took him to the doctor, who checked his leg and pronounced it fit. He cut the cast off, but warned Daniel to take it easy for another month. "No climbing trees or hard work," he advised. "A vacation wouldn't hurt," he added with a twinkling glance at Brittney. "Hawaii for two or three weeks would be nice."

Daniel nodded, his mood very strange. He was solemn and silent. He seemed to have a lot on his mind.

"I'm going home at the end of the week," she said as soon as they were in the truck and on their way to the cabin.

"No," he said.

"I have to find a real job." And forget this place and the man who wanted his freedom more than he wanted her. The easy tears gathered again. She managed to blink them away.

"I'll give you one," he said. He was suddenly very near her in the truck. "A lifetime position."

"Watch out for the gear," she said as he slid even closer.

"Aren't you going to ask what kind of position?"

She shook her head, her thoughts going around and around like a fast two-step. He made no sense at all. "Did you get another blow on the head?" she asked.

"No." He stroked her shoulder. "Tell me some more about marriage," he suggested in a husky voice.

She stole a look and saw the fire in his eyes. Her breath caught in her throat. No, she wasn't going to let him do this to her again. "There's nothing left to say."

"Then I'll have to tell you." He dropped an arm around her and rubbed her neck, slowly, sensually. It was driving her wild.

"Don't," she muttered, clenching her teeth against the ready response of her traitorous body.

"Making love is the one that comes first to mind," he said, his breath warm against her ear. "We'd be great together. You have such a natural passion, and I have such a hunger for you. We could show each other what feels best, learn each other's likes and dislikes...."

His voice trailed off, leaving her in a sensual haze of need and longing. "It wouldn't work," she said desperately. "I'd encroach on your space and tell you what to do. You'd get mad."

"No," he promised. "I've discovered it's natural to be concerned about someone you love." His tone changed. "I was terrified when you threw yourself at Limmer. Don't you ever do anything so stupid again."

She took her eyes off the road to peruse his expression. "I can't promise that."

He laughed suddenly. "Of course, you can't. When you see a need, you jump right in. Ah, Brittney, what wonderful fights we're going to have. And then we'll make up."

He nuzzled her ear and strewed hot kisses along her neck.

"Daniel," she protested. "I can't drive."

He waited until she turned off the main road onto the gravel one. As soon as they were around the bend and hidden by trees, he said, "Pull over and stop."

"No."

"Then we'll have a wreck." He bit her neck tenderly.

She stopped. Scrunching against the door, she demanded, "What has gotten into you? This...this isn't funny, Daniel." She swallowed. "Are you getting back at me for what I did to you?"

He didn't smile or look triumphant or anything she expected. "No, I'm trying to point out the advantages of marriage to me. You've already told me your views. I thought I should tell you mine."

She stared at him, at a loss for words.

"Let's see, we were talking about making love. I'd be a considerate lover. I'm a good provider, too. You wouldn't have to work unless you wanted to. If you do, there are plenty of jobs in the company. Or the part-time one at the museum."

He leaned close, letting her see deep into his eyes. The confusion and anger she'd felt faded. She saw passion, hot as the sun, shining there. Did she see more?

"Daniel?" she whispered.

He took her hand and pressed it against his chest. She felt his heart beating, steady and strong.

"A husband is a friend who lasts a lifetime," he continued, smiling slightly. But his mood was serious, not teasing. "A husband is a lover who's always there. You can give him all your passion with no holding back. You can trust him with your heart. A husband doesn't take unfair advantage. Isn't that right?"

She nodded. Tears came into her eyes, gathering on her long, beautiful lashes. He wiped them away with his thumb.

"Marriage means someone is there to look after you and help you when you're sick, to take your side when there's trouble. Like you did for me." He drew a ragged breath. "Say yes, kitten. I'm about to run out of reasons, and I want you so much."

"Are you asking me to marry you?" She wanted to make sure she understood. No more leaps in the dark.

"Absolutely."

She tried for a lighter mood. "About time," she said, then she put her head on his chest and burst into tears.

She heard his laughter as he rubbed his hand over her hair. "You are a continual surprise," he said. "Is that yes?"

She nodded, raised her face and kissed him. Endlessly. Passionately. Intimately. "We'll have such a wonderful life. You won't miss being alone. I'll give you room. I won't make demands—well, not too many...."

He kissed her. Endlessly. Passionately. Intimately. "We'll have to enlarge the cabin and add a few amenities for when we have kids," he said. "We'll stay here in the summer. Carol and Sonny can take over in town. We'll live at the lake house in winter."

Was she dreaming? "Yes," she said. "Carol and Sonny. Do you mean it?"

"We'll give them a try. They'll have to work their way p." He laughed again. "Do you want to go to Hawaii?"

"For our honeymoon? No. We'll be married as soon as 'arol gets home." She looked anxious. "Would you mind big wedding in Louisiana? My family will disown me if I on't give them that much. The governor will have to ome."

Daniel gazed at her with adoration. Brittney hadn't al- rays done what her folks wanted, but she had always con- dered them in her decisions. He didn't want her to change.

"I'd get married in hell if it would make you happy," he owed, gathering her into his arms.

"Why did you change your mind?" she asked.

"I realized there was nothing in my life that wouldn't be etter with you in it," he said.

It was the simple truth.

Brittney looked at him. It was all there: the passion, the evotion, all the love she could ever want.

"Daniel, the married man," she whispered, loving him so 1uch.

"Brittney's man," he corrected, helping himself to an- ther kiss.

MORE ABOUT
THE AQUARIUS MAN

by Lydia Le

Aquarians value friendship over romance. Let's just get that out in the open right away. We might as well add that the Water Bearer is downright suspicious of romance. However, the Uranus-ruled man *will* fall in love when he decides it's the sensible thing to do. It could also be said that Aquarian men are intrigued by a mystery and can be lured into a relationship once their curiosity has been aroused. It could seem to take forever, and just when you're about to pack your bags and look for a cuddly Taurus or a fiery Leo, your Aquarian will sweep you up in one of his unpredictable blasts of energy. Why, you might ask? Simple: Aquarians are ruled by both conventional Saturn *and* radical Uranus. Take your pick or better yet, combine them, stand back and wait for lots of surprises!

The Aquarian man loves surprises. He's the original beatnik. His eccentricity, free-spiritedness and freedom coupled with practicality, discipline and a patina of normalcy is both maddening *and* comforting. If you do find yourself drawn by his brand of unique chemistry, be prepared to have him forget all sorts of things—such as where he parked the car, put his keys, when and where you first net. Not to worry, this gem will remember the important things: he loves you and will *never* leave you. Infidelity is not the Aquarian's cup of tea, thank you very much. It is a fixed sign and, unless other factors in his chart indicate it, the Aquarian man is not likely to change his mind.

When the Aquarian finally does decide to make a commitment—though some of them do remain bachelors for life—he will look for a woman who can fill the role of wife-mother-mistress-confidant-secretary-and-pal! Sounds sexist? No, not really. This air sign—and contrary to popular misconception the Water Bearer *is* an air sign—will probably be found in the forefront of women's rights ... and animal rights and conservation and just about every other cause on the planet. Aquarians have their share of contradictions. So, if your Uranian lover wants you to play geisha for the evening, be willing to put down your Amazon shield and slip into a nice silk kimono. You will be amply rewarded, and it just might take all night.

Every man has an Achilles' heel, and Aquarian men are no exception. Simply put, it takes a long time for them to figure out who they are. Until they do, their sense of self is shaky. They cover this up by not letting you get too close. Like Sagittarians, their motto could easily be Don't Fence Me In. However, with the Aquarian man this refrain comes from his inability to be intimate with someone else when you haven't figured out your own identity. Even when he does, there will always be a certain coolness about the Uranian fire. Perhaps this is why Aquarian men are traditionally coupled with Leo women, known for their passion. Together they complement one another. This is not to say that other combinations don't work. They can and do; much depends on the individual horoscopes.

Perhaps the best advice for women dealing with Aquarian lovers is that a slow start, with friendship first and maybe more hand-holding than you thought possible in the 1990s, is your key to a long and richly rewarding loving relationship.

* * * * *

Famous Aquarian Men

James Dean
Clark Gable
Paul Newman
Telly Savalas
John Travolta
Burt Reynolds
Charles Dickens

Star-crossed lovers?
Or a match made in heaven?

Why are some heroes strong and silent . . . and others charming and cheerful? The answer is WRITTEN IN THE STARS!

Coming each month in 1991, Silhouette Romance presents you with a special love story written by one of your favorite authors—highlighting the hero's astrological sign! From January's sensible Capricorn to December's disarming Sagittarius, you'll meet a dozen dazzling and distinct heroes.

Twelve heavenly heroes . . . twelve wonderful Silhouette Romances destined to delight you. Look for one WRITTEN IN THE STARS title every month throughout 1991—only from Silhouette Romance.

STAR

Silhouette Special Edition

proudly presents
the long-awaited "prequel" volume of

★ **LOVE AND GLORY** ★
by
LINDSAY McKENNA
Dawn of Valor

In the summer of '89, Silhouette Special Edition premiered three novels celebrating America's men and women in uniform: LOVE AND GLORY, by bestselling author Lindsay McKenna. Featured were the proud Trayherns, a military family as bold and patriotic as the American flag—three siblings valiantly battling the threat of dishonor, determined to triumph . . . in love and glory.

Now, discover the roots of the Trayhern brand of courage, as parents Chase and Rachel relive their earliest heartstopping experiences of survival and indomitable love, in

Dawn of Valor, Silhouette Special Edition #649

This month, experience the thrill of LOVE AND GLORY—from the very beginning!

Available at your favorite retail outlet, or order your copy by sending your name, address, zip or postal code, along with a check or money order (please do not send cash) for $2.95, plus 75¢ postage and handling, payable to Silhouette Reader Service to:

In the U.S.
3010 Walden Ave.
P.O. Box 1396
Buffalo, NY 14269-1396

In Canada
P.O. Box 609
Fort Erie, Ontario
L2A 5X3

Please specify book title with your order. Canadian residents add applicable federal and provincial taxes.

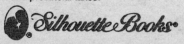

Silhouette Books®

DV-1A

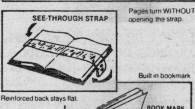

SILHOUETTE·INTIMATE·MOMENTS®

WELCOME TO
FEBRUARY
FROLICS!

This month, we've got a special treat in store for you: four terrific books written by four brand-new authors! From sunny California to North Dakota's frozen plains, they'll whisk you away to a world of romance and adventure.

Look for

L.A. HEAT (IM #369) by Rebecca Daniels
AN OFFICER AND A GENTLEMAN (IM #370) by Rachel Lee
HUNTER'S WAY (IM #371) by Justine Davis
DANGEROUS BARGAIN (IM #372) by Kathryn Stewart

They're all part of February Frolics, available now from Silhouette Intimate Moments—where life is exciting and dreams do come true.

FF-1A

Silhouette Books®

SILHOUETTE·INTIMATE·MOMENTS®

NORA ROBERTS
Night Shadow

eople all over the city of Urbana were asking, Who was that masked
an?

ssistant district attorney Deborah O'Roarke was the first to learn
is secret identity . . . and her life would never be the same.

he stories of the lives and loves of the O'Roarke sisters began in
anuary 1991 with NIGHT SHIFT, Silhouette Intimate Moments
365. And if you want to know more about Deborah and the man
ehind the mask, look for NIGHT SHADOW, Silhouette Intimate
loments #373, available in March at your favorite retail outlet.

NITE-1

 *Silhouette Books*®